Lee Raven, Boy Thief

Zizou Corder is the not-so-secret-identity of Louisa Young and Isabel Adomakoh Young, who have been writing together since Isabel was seven. They have previously written three books together: the LIONBOY trilogy. They wander the world in a large blue canoe, and have 17 pet ducks as well as the lizard and the dead tortoise.

[author photo to follow]

Lee Raven, Boy Thief

Zizou Corder

Illustrated by — TBC

PUFFIN

PUFFIN BOOKS

Published by the Penguin Group

Penguin Books Ltd, 80 Strand, London WC2r 0rl, England

Penguin Group (USA) Inc., 375 Hudson Street, New York, New York 10014, USA

Penguin Group (Canada), 90 Eglinton Avenue East, Suite 700, Toronto, Ontario, Canada m4p 2y3

(a division of Pearson Penguin Canada Inc.)

Penguin Ireland, 25 St Stephen's Green, Dublin 2, Ireland (a division of Penguin Books Ltd)

Penguin Group (Australia), 250 Camberwell Road, Camberwell, Victoria 3124, Australia

(a division of Pearson Australia Group Pty Ltd)

Penguin Books India Pvt Ltd, 11 Community Centre, Panchsheel Park, New Delhi – 110 017, India

Penguin Group (NZ), 67 Apollo Drive, Rosedale, North Shore 0632, New Zealand

(a division of Pearson New Zealand Ltd)

Penguin Books (South Africa) (Pty) Ltd, 24 Sturdee Avenue, Rosebank, Johannesburg 2196, South Africa

Penguin Books Ltd, Registered Offices: 80 Strand, London WC2r 0rl, England

puffinbooks.com

First published 2008

1

Text copyright © Zizou Corder, 2008

Illustrations copyright © XXX, 2008

The moral right of the author and illustrator has been asserted

Set in Perpertua

Typeset by Palimpsest Book Production Limited, Grangemouth, Stirlingshire

Made and printed in England by Clays Ltd, St Ives plc

British Library Cataloguing in Publication Data

A CIP catalogue record for this book is available from the British Library

Isbn: 978-0-141-32290-2

For everyone who has ever found reading hard

ACKNOWLEDGEMENTS

Jack Fairbarn for inspiration, Ryan Lansley for encouragement, Ed Maggs for being so exceptionally gracious, the British Library, Derek Johns, and the usual mob.

CHAPTER 1

The Story According to Lee Raven, the Boy Thief

Earlier this year I got myself embroiled in an adventure so extremely peculiar and weird that if any other bloke had come up and told me it had happened to him I would've not believed him in fact I probably would've decked him for his cheek. However here I am sitting in the place to which this adventure brought me, with the purpose, prize and hero of the adventure in the hands of my friend beside me, so it must be true, and if you don't believe it I don't care because it don't matter, but don't try and deck me because if you do you'll be sorry.

I'll start at the beginning because I know that's where you ought to start a story. The beginning was, really, all that palaver in Greek Street, Soho, London, Great Britain, the UK, 20 April 2046, after the petrol ran out and the lowlands were drowned but before the Martians invaded (they still ain't yet, for your information, but you never know).

I, Lee Raven, useless git, pointless specimen, little oik, bliddy hoodie, thievin' ratbag (I'm merely quoting my fans

– well, my dad), thought what with it being Friday night and a sunny warm evening all orange with the dusk, there' be a load of guys the worse for booze out on the street in Soho and I'd go out and pick their pockets for them get me a bit of tosh and they'd never even know, probabl go home thinking they'd spent it all on booze. If they wa good blokes they'd have given it to charity for poor los homeless boys like me anyway, so I was just helping mysel direct. Plus I was saving them the ill-healthful effects c drinking that much extra that they would've drunk i they'd've had the money I'd nicked. So I was performin a public service of redistributing wealth and preventin public drunkenness.

So late in the evening I was waiting for them to star falling out of the pubs and clubs when I noticed a dye blonde bird in a fur coat and a very swanky handbag whic made me think she'd likely have a quite nice fat purs inside it, waiting outside that club with the duck on it. watched her for moment. She was on her own, and whe she turned I saw she had one of those faces covered i make-up to look young but underneath it was a face lik boiled meat. Probably she was waiting for someone t come out of the club. *Move fast, Lee-o*, I thought, so I swun by her and gave her the old brush and dip and 'Sorry Mrs!' as I passed. Only she only grabs my arm while I'n inside her bag, and holds it up in the air so's I'm on m toes, and she's yelling blue murder and anyone would'v thought I'd been trying to slit her throat not lift her caio — so then all these people are looking at us and some security come lurching out of the club and young Lee thinks, *All right, mate, enough of this,* so I kick her in the shins, extremely hard if I may say so, and she goes 'Eyurgh' and lets go of me to grab her leg, and I make off as quick as I can down the nearest revolting dark alleyway, which turned out to be the one where my aunt Jobisca lives since she had to leave Norfolk. Well, I wasn't going to stick around down there, so I roared off towards Piccadilly, looking for noise and crowds to hide in, only there was all the theatre and nightclub security along Shaftesbury Avenue, and I didn't fancy fighting my way past them, so I took a way towards Regent Street, and just kept on, feet thumping, heart thumping, keep going, and I crossed Regent Street all right and kept going and before long I was way out of my territory in a part of town I didn't know at all, so I kept *on* going just in case and after a while there was a big garden square so I pitched myself over the railings (One-handed! Legs flying!) and flung myself down under a big old bush and lay there, and my heart was beating so hard I could feel it juddering the hard earth beneath me.

Otherwise it was quiet except for a bird singing away.

No one had followed me. I thought I'd keep my head down anyway. No more running around tonight, that's for sure.

It was a good enough place to sleep. I tucked myself inside under the branches and the drooping leaves, and I pulled my jacket round me. The earth was hard and dry and crumbling against my cheek. London wormcasts. I'd wake up covered in little grey squiggles.

And I'd got her purse too, safe in the deep pocket my mum had sewed in the back of my jacket lining for just such a purpose.

So the next day, I was just entirely minding my own business. I'd woken quite late considering I was outdoors, and thanks to Mrs Wallet – she had a bunch of cash, but I hadn't been through it properly yet – I'd bought my coffee and a chocolate croissong and a cheese and ham toastie and a big raspberry sherbet. I took them all back under my bush in the square, and it was a bit sunny and some leaves and blossoms like soapsuds were out on the trees and the buildings were all tall and white and handsome, so I sat there feeling completely happy, as it happens, munching and feeling the sun on my nose. If the sun's out, I'm happy. It's that simple.

For about ten minutes.

Then a bloke came and sat on a bench along the way. I thought about dipping him but decided not – I'd enough for the moment, and it was too quiet and light, and I didn't feel like any more running away yet, not after last night. So I just ignored him.

He had a coffee and a sandwich, and looked like an

officeguy on his break. He was having a shufti at the paper – checking the results by the look of it.

I'd finished my food, so being a good citizen up I got and strolled over to the bin, which was behind him, to dump my wrappings.

And as I passed, I took a look at his paper. And got a bit of a shock. There on the front page was a picture – big picture – of me. You wouldn't necessarily see it was me as my face was half hidden but I recognized myself – I've got this pretty weirdly pale hair – and I recognized the bird in the fur all right and there was my hand and it was pretty blatant what was going on. There was a big old headline and a load of writing to the side.

The officeguy noticed me standing there like a lemon because he looked up and smiled at me and looked down at the story, and said, 'Yeah! Romana Asteriosy got mugged last night! Amazing, isn't it? The amount of security she'd have and she got mugged by a kid! Pity that kid . . .'

Well that was enough. I tried to sort of grin and nod to cover up my dropped jaw, and moved on, and dumped my wrapping, and kept on moving.

Romana Asteriosy! Well that explains the amount of security that jumped out on me.

Romana Asteriosy is only one of the richest of the Rich Russians in London. I don't think she's actually Russian though. She owns half the shops and half the football teams and crike knows what. Extremely rich and dodgy as all crike. You can't blame me for not recognizing her though – she's never photographed, except sometimes in shades. She's too mysterious for photographs. 'A shadowy figure', they call her on the TV.

But I never mugged her! I dipped her. It's different. I didn't threaten her. I didn't hit her. I don't carry – I don't like it. I just nicked her bliddy purse.

I felt the weight of it in my jacket.

I had to get rid of it, certes.

I looked round for a private place. Bogs in the cafe would do.

I went back there, ordered another sherbet and went into the toilet. Locked in the stall, I took out the purse and checked through the tosh properly.

It was the fold-out wallet kind. Full of caio, as I said. Three hundred dirhams! More than I'd seen – in my life, actually. The richness of some people – my mum could've fed us all for a month on that. Well, I was keeping it. I took it out and stuffed it in my inside pocket.

Cards: five, cash and debit and credit and all that. I wasn't interested in cards. Too much technology and no way you can use them and stay safe. I know some people sell them on and stuff but it's too complicated for me. I ain't mixing with that kind of people – once you've done business with them they think they own you and the next thing you know you're sharing a room with a dozen kids brought in a box from god knows where, none of them talk English, they're crying all night and you're all getting beat up. No thank you. I only want clean anonymous stuff I can use – cash caio.

Photos: an old one of a guy in glasses – twentieth-century-looking. Probably her husband or her dad or something. Well, for sure I didn't need anybody else's family.

ID card, driving licence, some other stuff. None of it was anything to me. She was welcome to it. I'd jump a tube train out to Clapham or somewhere and leave it somewhere, and it could do what it wanted.

That's what I was doing. I came out of the cafe and walked down the square towards the tube station at Green Park. And walking up towards me was a bunch of security. I don't know whose, or where they were from, but they had that look of importance like they were Doing Something, and in a split second my mind went off on one and I knew for a fact that they were Asteriosy's security, and what they were doing was looking for me, and here I was with the wallet in my pocket, just walking up to them like a dork . . .

The houses in that section are very grand, tall and old with the blue plaques on their fronts about all the grand blokes who used to live there

I ducked up the nearest set of steps leading up to a front door.

I didn't even know who lived here or what. There was a big brass sign, and glass windows in the door. *Very* grand. Inside I could see a wide hall, and bookshelves.

Behind me, the security glanced up at me, semi-interested, from the other side of the street. One of them slowed down. He stopped to tie his shoe. The others stood around, with nothing better to do than stare at me.

There was a smaller brass plate by the doorbell. I stared at it. It might well say on it 'Deliveries to the basement door please'. I put a look on my face as if that had been what I just read, and then strolled down the stairs, innocent as you like, and down the much smaller and less glam set of stairs into the area where the basement door was. Out of their view so I wouldn't have to a) stand there like a lemon or b) ring! Clever, eh?

The only problem was, they were also out of my view so I had no idea whether they had finished tying their shoes yet and gone on about their business, or whether they were looking at their photo and discussing how the pale-headed kid in it looked exactly like the pale-headed kid they'd just seen going down the stairs looking dodgy.

So I had to stay down there for a bit.

So I did.

Then it started raining.

It was all right because there was a kind of arch under the stairs up to the front door, so I went in under there, where the coal hole was in Victorian times.

I'd been there a while, leaning against the whitewash

and congratulating myself on a lucky escape, when a face stuck itself up against the wire glass in the basement door, and a great rattling began, and the door shot open.

It was an old geezer – tall, stooping, in a dark suit and a big thick moustache. He was already talking: '. . . because if you'd rung someone should've come, I'd have thought, rather than leave you out in the rain, poor blighter, come in, come in. I was upstairs and didn't hear, lucky I came down actually. I was looking at the letters of David Docherty . . . I don't suppose you know him – very highly thought of in the late twentieth but hardly known now, still terribly funny though I don't know what I'm going to do with them . . .'

I took one look at him and saw something to be turned to my advantage.

'David Docherty who wrote *The Cannibal Death*, sir?' I chirped up in my best polite voice.

He'd been ushering me but now he stopped and turned to me. 'Yes!' he cried. 'Have you read him?'

Yeah. Well. That's the question that floors me. Have you read . . .?

I didn't answer him.

I didn't say the truth, which was, *No, I bliddy haven't because I can't bliddy read.*

I can catch a rat by the tail just by sneaking up on it, I can pick pockets like the Dodger and filch off market stalls and run like a cat, I can swear in several languages and add things up in my head and I remember everything that I ever hear or see, but I can't read.

That's why the teacher told Dad I was DYS LEX IC and needed help. That's why I wouldn't go to school. My dad thought it meant I was STU PID PRAT and should be thwacked till I saw sense.

That's why I left home.

I didn't run away, mind. I'm not some little coward. I escaped.

Anyway, so I said, 'Yeah. Brilliant. Really scary, ain't it, that bit when . . .'

I knew all about it because my brothers used to watch the old film. They wouldn't let me watch because they said I was too little but then they'd scare me with stories about how this guy was going to eat me up and all of that. Ciaran was the worst. He'd go on and on: 'He'll slice out your liver and fry it with onions, he'll get chips from the chippy and a big bottle of beer, he'll deep-fry your fingers and put mustard on you and ketchup . . .' and Finn would grab me from behind, going, 'YUM-YUMYUM', and Billy and Squidge would laugh at us and tell us to shut up and in the end Dad would come in and yell.

The old geezer was saying, 'I never read *The Cannibal Death*. Do you know, I found it simply too frightening. Had to put it down. I don't find that kind of thing amusing any more, at my age . . . So – do come on in.'

Come on in? All right. Don't mind if I do.

'Yeah – ta.' I said. Bye-bye, blokeys outside. Lee's been admitted, and by that fact is proved an innocent Lee, going about innocent business. Bye.

The building smelt funny. Dusty and leathery and old. Not quite damp. Chilly and warm at the same time. The floor was big old stone slabs, like we were in a garden or on the pavement still, and there were all these bookcases everywhere, and books just piled all over the place: really old-looking ones mostly. I don't like books. They've got everything in them, and I can't get at it.

On one set of shelves they were all a kind of ghostly white, like pearl. He caught me looking at them and said, 'Ah, our vellum collection.' I nodded wisely as if I knew all about it, and stored the word away for when I could find out.

'You'll like this,' he said suddenly, and grabbed me and pulled me towards what looked like a big, thin, tightly rolled leather carpet.

'Eighteenth-century deerskin,' he said. 'Shipwrecked!'

'Yer what?' I replied.

'This is a roll of deerskin from the eighteenth century,' he said. 'It was on a ship going from Spain to New York, and the ship was wrecked.'

'Why ain't it all rotted away?' I asked.

'The right question!' he said, gleaming. 'It was so tightly rolled, and so tightly packed in, that the water never got to it. It was salvaged in the early 2000s and found to be in perfect condition. Sniff it.'

I sniffed it. Leather, age – and salt.

'Isn't it beautiful?' he said.

He had a funny face – great big curving nostrils and eyes like under-cooked poached eggs and a moustache like someone had parked a broom up his nose – but I was quite liking him. Not that it was going to be able to last long – I knew that.

He took me into, of all things, a kitchen, tucked away among more rooms full of books. It had no windows, an old pale green table and lino on the floor. There was a hot pot of tea on the table and a packet of HobNobs.

'You're all wet,' he said. 'Would you like a cup of tea?'

This did surprise me. Then he looked at me again.

'You're *not* the lad from the auctioneers, are you?' he said.

'No,' I said.

He seemed mildly disappointed.

'And why were you here then, in my basement?' he asked.

'Just keeping out of the rain,' I said, looking all blue-eyed and innocent. It's a look I have had to perfect.

'Do your parents know where you are?'

Uh-oh. Here it comes – the lecture, the load of sympathy, the handing over of the miscreant to the authorities.

'Yeah of course I'd best be on my way then thanks for

the biscuits,' I said hurriedly, and jumped up, and legged it. I was quicker than him and off out of there – or at least I would have been, and I would've made it too, only no one but a criking homing pigeon could've found his way out of that maze of a building. I thought I'd just gone back the way we came, but one shelf of books looks a lot like another and I think I turned left at the vellum not right, and the next thing I had to go up a skinny little staircase because Mr Whoever-he-was was right behind me, rustling about like a ferret up a hole, because he'd taken some shortcut. Anyway, so I was up these stairs and down a corridor and then pushing through a big, solid, heavy door – and suddenly we're in another country. Thick green carpets. Reverential hush. High ceilings and a big old chandelier dangling. Windows down to the floor. Bliddy great marble fireplace over there. Swankerama, old-school style. It looked like a historical telly programme.

I slowed down and tried to look like I belonged, in case there was anyone to see me. Sauntered towards a big pair of double doors, leading I hoped perhaps to the front door back on to the square.

Suddenly Mr Thing leapt out of a door in front of me. 'Hold on,' he said. 'You can't get out that way. Come with me.'

He was making me nervous. I overreacted, I know that now. But he was blocking my way and not letting me out and it was making me . . . nervous.

So I pushed past him.

And he pushed me back.

Well I could've clocked him, but he was old and I don't like clocking old people. Doesn't seem fair. I was about to do it anyway, but he'd got the advantage of my hesitating. With a quick movement, he shoved me through the door out of which he had just popped.

'Now just stay there while I decide what to do with you,' he said, as he slammed it shut on me.

It was the sheer surprise of it that let him get away with it. I was taken off guard, otherwise he'd never have achieved such a thing.

'Oi!' I yelled. 'Oi! You can't do that! Oi! Let me out! Let me out, you old sod!'

Nothing doing. Well, he was going to go to the Authorities, at a guess, wasn't he? Otherwise he would've just let me go. He was going to get somebody in who'd do me for assault and theft and take me home and my mum would cry and my dad would thwack me and I'd be in prison or, worse, back at school and everyone would be criking me out about being Stu Pid Prat just because I can't read and then I'd run away again. Big deal.

So I looked around. I was back in skinny-corridor-land by the looks of it. It was a decent-size room, shelves to the ceiling on all the walls, piles of old books everywhere, one lamp hanging on a bit of wire, a rackety ladder thing on wheels, no doubt for climbing up and down the shelves.

No windows. Another door, set in among the shelves: locked. In the corner was a little sink, and in the middle a chair in front of a big desk, with a computer on it – the only modern-looking thing in the place. I sat in the chair and whirled it round for a bit, but there's a limit to how long you can find that amusing. I took out Mrs Asteriosy's wallet and had a look through it again. I sighed a couple of times and looked round. On the shelf was a safe. I picked it just for fun, for something to do. Honest – I had no intention of nicking nothing. I was just stuck in a boring bliddy room with crike all to do, so I was amusing myself like anyone would.

Inside, there was a metal briefcase – tigrenium, if I wasn't mistaken. I recognized the metal because my dad always made me look out for it. It's very light and very strong. You could bash away for hours and not make a dent, and you can't cut it. They use it for safes and stuff. Only valuable items get stored in tigrenium. So you notice it.

Well, because it was tigrenium, and in a safe, I opened it. Course I did. Inside was lined with soft red furry velvety stuff, and lying on the stuff like a movie star in her bath was – the *Beano Annual*.

Well, I like the *Beano*. The only time we ever had anything like books at home was when Mum decided one time when we were little that she should read us bedtime stories, so she got this copy of the *Beano* and read Dennis the Menace to us. She read that same copy over and over, and we all laughed at the stupid dad running round with his stupid slipper and Dennis getting one over on him the whole time.

I picked it up. On the cover was the Bash Street Kids, with a big picture of Plug, who my brothers always said looked like me. Or I looked like him. Plug Ugly. I like Plug.

There was a sort of honey and oranges smell in the office.

I opened it. The first strip was Dennis the Menace. There he was in his black and red stripy jumper, and there was Gnasher jumping up, and Dad . . . I smiled, and followed the pictures.

My heart kind of bounced.

How extremely peculiar.

It was the same story. The same strip my mum used to read, over and over . . .

I followed it with a strange sad kind of warmth growing up inside me. It was so lovely to see it. It made me feel like a little kid again, with Mum with her arm round me, and all of us being quiet and not fighting each other for once . . .

Dad burned our old *Beano*. He came in one time while we were looking at it for the ninety-ninth time with Mum and he thought we were laughing at him – well, we were – so he tore it in half and chucked it in the fire.

And here it was again. The exact same story. I started

laughing – a little hiccuppy laugh that might bring a tear with it if you were girly. Which I ain't. But I was really happy to see that Dennis the Menace story again.

And then I heard a whispering at the keyhole.

I whipped round, in one movement shoving the book under my jacket and twitching the lid of the box shut.

'Boy!' it said. It was the old geezer.

'What,' I said crossly. I swung the safe door shut with my elbow.

The key rattled. The book slipped as of its own accord into my thieves' pocket. The door opened. The old guy slid in and shut it behind him again.

'What's your name?'

'Joe English,' I said. It ain't. My name is Lee Raven. Joe English is what I use.

'And you're what – twelve? Fourteen?'

'That kind of thing,' I said.

'Well, Joe, my name is Edward Maggs, and this is my family business, and I can't help noticing that you are dreadfully grubby and quite possibly a street child – are you?'

'I live my own life,' I said, with some dignity, though I say so myself.

'Are you in trouble?'

I was a bit surprised by this. How could he tell?

'Those men who were approaching who caused you to enter my basement – were they after you?' He almost hissed this bit, though there was no one to overhear us.

'Certainly not,' I said.

'I thought so. They don't belong around here. I assume you have some skill in nefarious activity,' he said.

I just looked at him.

'The kind a person of tender years might have to acquire to survive on these mean streets . . .'

His square didn't look very mean to me, I can tell you. Not compared with some of the bailiwicks around which I've lurked.

'Could be,' I said.

He stared at me. I knew the expression on his face. I get it all the time. He was a decent old sod and didn't know whether to pity me or call security. Was I a poor boy struggling to get by as best he could in a wicked world, or was I a wicked boy who ought by rights to be locked up toot sweet?

And suddenly, as if he'd made up his mind, he announced, 'Off you go, young fellow, off you go, and don't come round my basement again. Don't know what you're up to, don't need to, not my business.'

He'd opened the door, and lugged me out into the hall, and was opening the front door. 'Off you go,' he said again, and chucked me down the stairs.

The blokeys, and just as well, had gone. I was all alone, stumbling out of the garden and collapsing on the pavement, picking myself up, brushing my knees and controlling a very strong urge to rush back up there and shout, 'Oi! What's all that about! First you lock me in, then you chuck me out . . . What's your problem?'

But he was right. We were not each other's business. My business was to get rid of this flamin' wallet –

Oh.

Patting myself down, the flaming wallet was not where it had previously been and should still be, i.e. in my thieves' pocket.

The flaming wallet was not on the pavement, not in the gutter. Nor on the stairs.

I scrabbled myself across the road and back under my preferred bush. I took off my jacket, checked all pockets and down the seat of my pants, and in my shoes, where I sometimes hide things, though it was pretty obvious it wasn't there as it was too darn big.

Nothing – except that *Beano* book, which I hadn't even meant to nick.

I knew all along where the wallet was. It was where I had left it – on Mr Maggs's desk.

So I swore for a bit, and I tightened up my mouth so it probably looked like a bumhole which is how it goes when I am really criked off, and I breathed hard and thought.

I had the caio at least. That was good.

But the old guy would find the wallet and realize it was Asteriosy's and realize I had left it and call the Authorities and they'd get a cracking description of me and my life would not be worth living, plus he'd see the *Beano Annual* was missing, with like my signature practically written all over the crime, and even though it was only a *Beano Annual* it had been in a tigrenium case, in a safe, so someone thought it was worth something, and the public police and Asteriosy's security would be all over me.

My first thought, which lasted a while, was I had to get back in there to Maggsland and nick back that wallet. Before he found it.

I groaned.

I hate housebreaking now. Too complicated.

I used to do it when I was little but I never thought about it then. It was just what we did. Normal. It was always the littlest kid's job in our family – going through the window and opening up for Dad to come through the door. I was the youngest in our family so it stayed my job for longest. I'd been proud at first when Finn got moved on for being too big. Dad talked it up like it was a real honour. There's only three things Ravens are any good at, toshing, flushing and nicking, and Dad made us proud.

But it was scary when you were only a tyke, and it's all dark in front of you and you don't know what's there, dogs maybe or alarms, or people – and Dad behind shoving yer and saying . . . what he said . . . and you go head first on the floor if you're not lucky.

But I was good at it. It's like falling off a bicycle – you don't forget how.

So I'd just go round and nick the wallet back.

I still had the peculiarly precious *Beano Annual* as well. Stupid bliddy instinct I got for pocketing stuff. Now what was I going to do with it?

CHAPTER 2

The Story According to Mr Maggs, the Bookseller

I have to say that the presence of the boy in the basement confused me. I assumed he had come from Christie's to pick up the copy of Johnson's Compleat History of the Pyrates for Mrs Netherby. True, he wasn't the usual boy, but they could have employed a new one. True, he didn't, once I had a proper look at him, resemble a Christie's boy: he was so pale, with his pale sticky-up hair and the bags under his eyes. He looked as if in his entire life he'd consumed nothing but chips and cheap lemonade. I was discombobulated by his presence, to tell the truth, particularly as it followed on so swiftly from my other two unusual visitors.

But I run ahead. My name is Edward Maggs, of Maggs Brothers Antiquarian Booksellers of Berkeley Square. I am absolutely accustomed to handling rare and valuable items. We have vaults for humidifying and dehumidifying, to rehydrate a brittle book or dry out a damp one. We have contraptions with dry-glove fingers which will turn the pages of ancient documents so that the paper is not damaged by contact with the chemicals and moisture of human skin. We have volumes worth thousands, millions of dirhams. We have lights that cast no light, so that exquisite illuminations made by monks a thousand years ago can be rendered visible without being harmed by the presence of actual light. We can salvage ancient leathers and vellums, redeem shattered spines with new strength, reattach prodigal pages. My confidence in all of this is unshakeable. My family has been doing these things since 1721.

But this news . . . this latest arrival . . . and the consequences . . . I was deeply perturbed.

A man had come only the night before.

It was late when he knocked at the door. It had been a bright spring day but with evening a fog had drawn in, and the street lamps gave a sulphurous gloomy light to the square, through which the blossoming trees glowed and loomed like ghosts. Nobody was about. I would normally have retired by that hour to the rooms on the top floor where I make my habitation, but on this evening I happened to be studying the accounts in my office downstairs.

He knocked at the front — I thought at the time, why did he not use the bell? — and I turned to the security camera, wondering who had come so late. Seeing a reputable-looking gentleman in his forties, in a hat, with a metal briefcase, I went to the front and spoke to him through the communication system.

His name was Ernesto de Saloman. He was sorry to call so late. He had, he said, arrived recently from Paris. He had he said, a book so valuable that it could not be kept at home even in a safe. It was under his arm. Could he come in?

I was accustomed to keeping items of value on behalf of their owners. His name was familiar to me as a biblio phile, one who bought and sold and loved books although I was not acquainted with him personally. admitted him.

Once within, he removed his hat and shook from it the vestiges of damp and fog. His dark hair lay flattened to his handsome head, and his sallow complexion told of weariness and worry. I led him to my study – the rest of the emporium being closed up for the night – and asked him what it was he had.

'An old French manuscript,' he said, 'dealing with the myths and legends of Mesopotamia.'

'What date?' I asked, eyeing the briefcase, which was made of metal and seemed very large and strong for one old French manuscript.

'1799,' he replied, and perhaps I looked surprised. could not imagine how such a thing could be so valuable It was not my area of specialist knowledge but – well there were many books published in French at that time It may be worth several thousand, but it was not, at first description, a priceless item.

'May I look?' I asked – and he stopped me.

'This book may not be looked at,' he said.

I raised my eyebrows.

'Look instead at this letter, which accompanies the book.'

He placed it on my desk – a yellowed, dry fold of paper. I did not lower my eyebrows.

'Even I, its owner, have never looked at this book,' he said, as if by way of reassurance. I could hardly believe anything so peculiar, but his dark, tired eyes showed nothing but sincerity.

I went to the basin I keep in the corner of my study for just such a purpose, and washed and dried my hands carefully. Opening a small drawer, I found a pair of reading gloves and put them on before picking up the letter and delicately unfolding it.

In a spidery hand typical of the date, faded and brown, it read thus:

Messieurs,

A cause de ce livre, ma tante est morte et ma mère est folle. C'est un objet plein de larmes, de tristesse, de danger et de désespoir. On ne peut pas le détruire – il ne faut pas le lire.

Croyez moi qui connaît.[*]

---

[*] Sirs, Because of this book, my aunt is dead and my mother mad. It is a thing full of tears, of sadness, of danger and of despair. It cannot be destroyed – it must not be read. Believe me, one who knows.

It was signed with a grand illegible flourish, and the name written out beneath was Marianne de la Roche Lambert Limonov.

I folded the letter again and returned it to Mr de Saloman.

'Most bizarre,' I commented. 'Have you respected the stipulations of this letter?'

'I have,' he replied.

'Why?' I had to ask, although it was scarcely polite.

'Because I respect the woman who passed the instruction on to me,' he said firmly. 'My grandmother.'

'And are you asking me to keep this book for you?'

'I am,' he replied courteously. 'It has been in danger – it is in danger! – and must stay somewhere safe.'

'Can you not keep it at home?'

'At home!' he laughed shortly. 'Least of all there . . .' And a look of great sadness passed across his face.

'Take it to the bank,' I said, I fear a trifle curtly. 'I cannot offer a home to a book I may not examine.'

His face was troubled. 'I know,' he said urgently, 'that under normal circumstances you would need to collate the book, to make sure that it is complete, so that you can record exactly what it is you have accepted. But please . . .' Here he glanced briefly over his shoulder in a nervous fashion, a gesture which seemed to me – how wrong I was! – to be of calculated melodrama. 'Please, take this book. I will write you a letter absolving you of any responsibility for the number of pages. I trust you. My father dealt with your father, and his father with his. All I ask is that you place it between other books, keep it, and tell no one.'

Though he was by complexion a sallow man, his face was almost moonlight pale, with a light sheen of feverish sweat over it. Something was frightening him.

'If this book is so important to you,' I asked, 'why do you not take it to someone you know? Or, as I said, to a bank, designed specifically for guarding items of value?'

He just shook his head wearily. 'I trust no one,' he said. 'I have been deceived, and by one who above all should have my trust . . . This is why I have to trust a stranger. God knows, don't you think I would rather do this any other way? Just keep it,' he said, pressing the case into my hands, 'until I return.'

I resisted his offering – but it was futile. I could no more let a rare book drop to the ground than a nurse could a baby. I found myself taking it from him, and as I did so he was retreating from me, his arms still out in front of him, pressing the briefcase to me, smiling tiredly and saying, 'Just until I return. Just until I return.'

And he was gone. The door closed behind him, and until I had put the case down – it was bulky enough to occupy both my hands – I could not pursue him. By the time I could, it was too late. I heard the front door swing slowly shut; heard the echo of running feet down the steps to the square, and he had vanished into the night

I returned to my study, sat at my desk and stared at Monsieur de Saloman's metal briefcase. It was tigrenium I realized. For precious things.

I sighed, fetched myself a small glass of whisky, and opened the case.

It was lined with padded velvet, no doubt for protection. The book within was foolscap size. Its binding was certainly unusual: a rough vellum with a curious tooled and printed design. It could, at first glance, have been French, and late eighteenth century – but it could have been made at almost any time. It looked home-made, to tell the truth. Its spine was loose, I could see, and there was a lot of wear and tear, but it seemed strong, in decent condition.

Only for a second did Monsieur de Saloman's instruction on no account to look at it cross my mind as I picked it up.

The paper was rather foxed, there were no identifiable endpapers . . . no publisher's mark or title page – almost certainly hand-bound, by an amateur, not that well.

I glanced inside. Unlike some book dealers, I am quite interested in what is written on the page, as well as the provenance and value and edition and condition and so on.

Well, Monsieur de Saloman certainly hadn't ever looked at the book. Or he was either mad or lying or having some peculiar little joke. This wasn't an account of Mesopotamian myths and legends. It wasn't even in French. It was . . .

How can I say?

My heart beats faster now even to think of it. Of what it seemed as if it might be.

It was handwritten in English, in a fair secretary hand – taught in all the grammar schools at end of the sixteenth century. I can't read that script fluently, with its ligatured letters and annoying abbreviations, which could be anything – but I can pick things out.

In the front of the book, it said 'Mortlake, 1603–4, House of Ag. Phllps'.

It was set out in paragraphs, dated. It looked like a diary.

Words jumped out at me: 'Her Maiesties death'; 'Mr Johnson calls for me'; 'My Ladie Pembroke inuites to Wilton . . . her son refuses still to marry . . .'

I gulped.

'In the scilens here my mind wanders freely . . . looking again at Boccaccio . . .'

The date was right. The place was right.

On the opening front page was written: 'Librum Wm Shkspr'.

Oh, lord, it could not be, it could not be.

But it looked like . . .

Oh, lord, it looked so like . . .

Shakespeare kept no diary. Shakespeare's diary is Atlantis El Dorado, the Philosopher's Stone, the Holy Grail. These are not things you find in a box on your desk.

Queen Elizabeth died in 1603. Augustine Phillips was one of Shakespeare's players.

Oh, lord . . . oh, lord.

I quickly availed myself of the Internet.

The Internet told me that there was plague in London in 1603, and even before the Queen's death the theatres were closed to prevent it spreading further. Shakespeare and his company went out of town to wait for it to clear. To Mortlake, to Augustine Phillips's house.

But that proves nothing. Any forger could know this.

In 1603 Shakespeare wrote *All's Well That Ends Well*. It is based on a story from Boccaccio. The young earl, Bertram, refuses to marry.

Mary Sidney, Lady Pembroke, invited Shakespeare to stay at Wilton at that time.

Any forger could find these things out . . .

But even as a forgery, what quality! It would be almost contemporaneous!

I was beside myself with excitement. It was all I could do to prevent myself from ringing Mr Maud, the palaeographer, at Cambridge. I would not speak to the great Shakespeare scholars yet. First speak to the handwriting expert, and to the . . . No! Freddy, our seventeenth-century specialist, is coming in tomorrow. First of all I will show it to him. We must first of all confirm the age of the document. Be calm, Maggs. We do not yet know what this is.

Oh, my giddy aunt.

I sat up very late staring at the pages. The hooked aitches seemed to dance across the page. Finally, very tenderly, I put the book back in its box and shut the lid. I put it in my safe, locked it, and went up to bed.

Interlude

The tough little grey mice snuck out as soon as the old man had gone to bed.

One led a small posse across the floor to the bookshelf. It was no trouble for them to scrabble silently up to where the safe was. Perched easily on another's shoulders, she put her ear to the wheel of the safe and listened. Her tiny pink claws clutched at the dial and two others pulled on her tail when she needed extra strength. They worked like clockwork, a stream of efficiency, a team that needed no words, no instructions. Like cells in body, leaves on a branch, they were many parts adding up to one whole.

The safe door swung open.

The mice stood respectfully in the opening and gazed at the book.

Then, all together, they spoke some words in a language so ancient even they didn't understand them. They were the words that had to be said. That was all they knew. They bowed their heads. They locked the safe again. They disappeared into the shadows.

CHAPTER 3

The Story According to Janaki, Mr Maggs's Assistant

The very next morning Mr Maggs's second peculiar visitor came.

I knew about Mr de Saloman turning up because although Mr Maggs is a fine, honourable, good man he doesn't always remember what's what and he gets his words in the wrong order from time to time, so I keep an eye on him. As soon as the knock came on the door in the middle of last night I was down there to deal with it in case he'd gone to bed, but he beat me to it, so I just hung about to hear what it was, and didn't go back upstairs till Mr de Saloman had left. It's not nosy of me. It's responsible. Someone's got to keep track.

The next morning I was up before him, opening the emporium, bringing in the milk and the post, and all that. When the bell rang, I assumed it was someone arriving early for work. Mr Nobbs-Jones, perhaps, the incunabulist, who was always prompt and was perhaps today even more so than usual. I disarmed the alarm system that covers the main part of the building (I'd already done the apartment's one – my little room is there by Mr Maggs's, so that was the first thing to do), drew back the long bolts of the front door and unlocked it with the great old key. Picking up the post from the hall floor, opening the door and saying 'Good morning' kept me occupied so that I did not immediately notice that this was not Mr Nobbs-Jones, nor yet Mrs Sykes, nor Freddy Llewellyn, nor Lady Ursula, who deals with music. It was in fact a young girl, about my own age, in a velvet cloak.

'Mr Maggs?' she said cheerfully and politely. 'Is he in?'

She seemed rather pert.

I peered at her, first through my glasses, then over them. I didn't know her.

'Yes?' I said, in a not very welcoming tone.

'Good morning!' she said. 'I've come for Mr de Saloman's book.'

Her cheeks were clear and pink, her hair bright and bouncy under her hood. You never saw such a healthy virtuous-looking girl. And yet, within this one sight of her I trusted her not an inch.

'And you are?' I said.

'Jenny Maple,' she said. For a moment I thought she made a little bob, like a Victorian child.

Jenny Maple! Nonsense. No one could be called Jenny Maple.

'Has Mr de Saloman sent you?' I asked.

'Of course,' she said. She held out a letter in her clean pink paw.

I accepted it and turned away slightly to read it.

'It's addressed to Mr Maggs,' she pointed out.

'I,' I said rather grandly, 'am Mr Maggs's assistant. I deal with all his correspondence.'

The letter read:

Dear Mr Maggs,

Thank you for keeping my volume on Mesopotamian myths. If you could now pass it on to Miss Jenny Maple I would be most grateful, as I am for your generous hospitality in looking after it. Please forward your bill to me at the Hôtel de Crillon, Paris.

With thanks,

Ernesto de Saloman

I folded it up again. 'I'll take it to Mr Maggs,' I said. 'He's not available at the moment.' (Of course he wasn't. It was only 7.30 in the morning.) 'Perhaps you could call later.'

'Well, I'm meant to fetch the book immediately,' she said, looking a little worried. 'Mr de Saloman is leaving the country.'

I squinted at her.

'I'll see what I can do,' I said, and turned on my heel, and shut the door.

Before taking the letter to Mr Maggs, I went into his

office. I opened the safe and peeked in to check that the book was there, but there was no time to look at it properly, as I had something on my mind.

Mr Maggs is quite old-fashioned in his way. Almost everybody now uses texts and email and internal commchip systems, but Mr Maggs likes pen and paper, especially for his records. I went across what he likes to call his filing system – trying to maintain order there is one of my tasks – and attempted to locate in this paper labyrinth something that might pass as a file of correspondence from people whose names start with S.

By a miracle, there was a file, labelled S, in the drawer marked Correspondence. I took the file out and riffled through letters from shoemakers, about Shakespeare, to the Swedish ambassador and – ah yes – one from Ernesto de Saloman. I thought I'd remembered right. It was from several years ago, enquiring about a first edition of D. L. Flusfeder's *Man Kills Woman*.

The signature on it was nothing like that on the letter I held in my hand.

I was just thinking that I might just pack the girl off without bothering Mr Maggs about it, when I heard him come rustling in.

'Ah, Janaki,' he said. He was still wearing his silk dressing gown and carrying a cup of coffee. 'It's you. Couldn't think who would be in here. Bit early for filing, isn't it? Anyway, I wanted to talk to you . . . What's that letter?'

So I showed it to him. Along with the old letter from Mr de Saloman. And told him about the girl on the doorstep.

'Little baggage!' he said. 'Who sent her? Bring her in — let's have a word with her.'

But when I returned to the doorstep, there was no one there. Which rather gave Mr Maggs and me to think as we ate our chocolate croissants. We had them there on the doorstep, as the sun had come out and it was still so early.

It was very pleasant, sitting there, looking out over the square.

Some people may think it peculiar that I live here with Mr Maggs, but because it is my only life, I find it normal. I should explain. Long ago, long before I was born, and when he was a young man, Mr Maggs won me in a poker game. My father was a particularly honourable man, in his own funny way, and when I eventually came into this world, he felt obliged to honour his debt. That's all. I can't suppose my mother liked it very much, but she died soon after. Sometimes I wonder about the life I might have had in the apricot-filled valleys of Kashmir. Very occasionally, I allow myself to wonder whether my mother might have lived longer had her baby not been taken away. But it doesn't help anything to think like that.

Mr Maggs, so he tells me, was delighted to have me because he had himself been lost at cards as a boy and as

a result had spent several very happy years in the househol
of my great-uncle the Maharaja of Ratnapur. He makes
point of buying me dried Kashmiri apricots at Fortnum'.
I love Mr Maggs.

But I digress.

As we ate, Mr Maggs told me about Mr de Saloman
visit. I was glad he did, otherwise I would have had t
pretend not to know, and that would have been inconven
ent and difficult to maintain. He was much bemused b
the situation that had developed and he seemed ver
excited about something, though he did not mentio
what.

'So we have a book, which . . . which isn't what it
owner says it is, and we're not allowed to touch it, an
now someone has attempted to inveigle it from us!' h
said.

I agreed it was a bit peculiar. I was wondering whethe
to ask him more when the phone rang, and it was his ca
from Hong Kong. Then he was very anxious to speak t
Freddy, who wasn't coming in till after lunch, and mear
while everybody started to arrive, and he had to have
meeting. At around quarter to nine I went off to the stud
in the back building, to get on with sorting the diarie
and letters of J. K. Rowling. (We'd recently acquired 24
boxes from her estate and I had only just begun.)

Around 12.30 lunchtime I went out to fetch some sand
wiches for Mr Maggs and I – grilled eel, from one of th

fish-stalls in Green Park. There seemed to be some sort of drama going on down there. The far end of the park had been roped off with blue and white striped police crime-scene tape, and there were rather a lot of policeguys around. I got that little dark feeling of thrill in my belly that you get when something dangerous or interesting is going on but you feel ashamed to be thrilled because somebody might be hurt. The stallguys were chatting in what I couldn't help noticing to be that tone of awe and interest and a touch of fear which denotes gossip of a ghoulish nature.

'Well, he hadn't been robbed,' said the cockleguy to the smoked fish guy.

'What about . . .' nudged the smoked fish guy.

'Not that I heard,' said the cockleguy.

'It's horrible,' said Mavis Ubsworth, who does the eels. 'You can't feel safe.' Then she caught sight of me and, following the logic that because I am young I mustn't be allowed to hear anything bad, even when I've already heard it, she put on a big fake smile and shouted, 'Your usual, dear? With lemon?'

It didn't matter anyway. The early edition of the evening paper was out as I came back on to Piccadilly with my sandwiches, and the placard outside the Ritz said in big black letters: MYSTERY OF GREEN PARK LAKE CORPSE.

Well. A corpse! In the park!

I bought a copy and stopped off for a moment on the

bench in Berkeley Square to scan the pages. I wanted to prepare how I told Mr Maggs. He sometimes got upset about things.

It's lucky I did.

The mystery corpse was of a gentleman in his forties, tall, sallow-skinned, foreign-looking and believed to be French by his coat and the sodden, bloodstained hat found nearby.

It was like a punch of shock to my heart.

I must go immediately to Mount Street and tell the police that it sounded very like Mr Ernesto de Saloman, bibliophile, of Paris . . .

But then I started thinking . . .

That girl who had come this morning . . .

When had the body been found?

It was only last night that . . .

The book!

This was all looking a bit complicated.

I must, unfortunately, speak to Mr Maggs.

CHAPTER 4

Continuing the Story According to Lee Raven

Well, I was pretty concerned about what I was going to do about this sniking wallet situation. For all I knew, Mr Maggs had found the wallet, missed the book and called the police already.

I could take the risk – nip straight back to the house, say I'd left the wallet, pick it up, drop the book and scarper. But I might already be too late.

And breaking in? It was a daft idea. One, they had serious security. Two, I for sure wasn't going in daylight and, three, by the time it was dark it would be way too late.

It all stank, frankly. I wasn't going in. Frankly, I was just going to have to leave the neighbourhood quickly and quietly. Just . . . scoot.

A girl with black polished hair was sitting on the bench people sit on to eat. She had a bag of grilled eels with her, which I could smell, and she was looking at a newspaper. When she'd gone, I'd up and leave.

Of a sudden, she gasped and her hand flickered, and

then she stared into space for a while. Then she got up and went across the road into Maggs's.

Thank crike I'd stayed under my bush. Otherwise she'd have seen me . . . I felt a bit ill. Time to leave, Lee. Just leave.

So I upped and headed for the Piccadilly end of the square, and down Curzon Street, where I looked across towards Green Park.

Piccadilly and the park were crawling with police. Crawling. Beyond the fish grills there was stripy tape between the trees, vans parked up, commchips going and rows of blokeys in white-paper boiler suits, walking very slowly and looking down at their big boots.

After my normal moment of panic — any time I see police I always think they're after me — it didn't take me long to cotton that they weren't there in their masses just because I'd dipped a wallet. Drastic as my crimes were, they didn't require fingertip searches by half the forces in London. I'd only kicked a dodgy old bird and nicked a wallet and lifted a *Beano Annual* by mistake. Even so, my heart gave a big splat and I did not want to amble down there and mix with them in a sociable fashion.

We'll be heading back up to Berkeley Square then. I took the other side, so no one would come roaring out of Maggs's at me. I slipped up Lansdowne Row, skirting the cafe tables and looking as if that had been what I was intending all the time, attempting to proceed swiftly but without calling attention to myself. Just a London lad, busy about his business. Head down. Leaving the neighbourhood.

Just past the Tropicana, a voice called my name.

Pause, or rush on? To rush on would invite comment. I looked back to see who it was being so untimely.

It was my brother Finn.

'Oi, Lee!' he yelled, cheerful and loud.

I would have been pleased to see him because he's all right, Finn. He's a bit older than me and not always the first off the line but he's not treacherous like some. I grabbed his arm and said, 'Voice down, man, I'm in trouble . . .'

He responded well and steered me up Bruton Lane, saying, 'So, what, was it you then?'

'Was it me then what?' I replied.

'Pushed the Frenchman into Rosamund's Pond?'

'What Frenchman?'

'Aintcha heard? There's a dead Frog in the pond.' He laughed a bit at his own joke, then got back to the more interesting thing of the mystery. 'This fella, in a fancy hat, found drowned, only they think he was dead when he went in. Right there in the pond . . .' Finn gestured behind him to where the Frenchman's watery grave lay, beyond Piccadilly, surrounded by peaceful green grass and police tape barriers.

'Parrently,' he continued, leaning in on me like everyone

was trying to listen to our important conversation but his words were for my lugs only, 'he'd been hanging round here last night in his hat, with a tigrenium case, Marco said, because he'd seen him, and had thought of clocking him for the case himself, only didn't because the fella was tall, and Marco is a little chicken, and anyway, while Marco was stalking him, he made a rather late visit to Maggs and when he came out he didn't have it no more – anyway, today Marco's full of how it would have been good luck for the Frog if Marco had done him, because then he might not have got topped, and how someone probably done him for the case, cos it had something fabulous in it only he didn't have it no more only they didn't know . . .'

Finn had a peculiarly unhelpful way of a telling a story but the sting of it was coming through loud and clear.

I was in trouble. Big trouble, big big trouble.

I had just stolen a *Beano Annual* for which apparently this guy had been murdered. So to add to police being after me – which they always are – and Mrs Asteriosy's top-of-the-range private Russian security being after me for nicking her purse, there was now a murderous person after this bliddy *Beano*, which I nicked by mistake.

But why in crike would anyone murder someone for a *Beano*?

Well, all right, I panicked a bit. My heart started going, higher and tighter and quicker, and my breathing was suddenly all out of time with it, and my shoulders went up round my lugs and I was retching with sickness, my stomach clutching and twisting itself, clutching and twisting.

'Whassup?' said Finn. 'Lee? You all right?'

I was bent double and gasping for breath. You would've thought he could see I was extremely not all right.

He put his hand nervously on my back.

'I got to hide,' I whispered. 'Got to hide me, Finn.'

I must have looked hideous enough for him to take me serious. For a moment I thought he was going to chat, or query, but he never – to his credit he just looked at me, blinked a couple of times, furrowed his brow and then said, 'Come on.'

He led me a couple of hundred yards further up. The moving steadied my breath a little. There was bins, a skip, some builders' detritus. It was some kind of maintenance area.

'Sit down a moment,' he said, and I did, curled up by the skip, and then he looked at me again and said, 'What's going on?'

Like I said, Finn's OK. But.

'I saw you in the paper this morning,' he said. 'Dipping Romana Asteriosy. You dork! Getting papped, dipping.'

'Exactly,' I said. I wasn't going to tell him that I had, in my pocket at that exact moment, what the Frenchman had been drowned for. 'Can't stick around here.'

'You sure?' he said again.

Looking over his shoulders, I saw a line of public police cross the end of the lane, heading up to Green Park. In the distance the sound of their sirens drifted over the everyday sounds of London in the spring as more of them arrived. Yeah, I was sure.

I nodded. My throat was too tight to utter.

We sat there a moment or two while I calmed down a bit. While calming, I thought. While thinking, I decided. It was not a nice decision but you don't always get nice in this life.

'I don't suppose,' I said, after a while, 'that you've got a skello?'

Finn stared at me. There's only one reason you'd want a skello, and it's not something very attractive or everyday.

'Have yer?' I asked.

'Lee,' he said, 'what you thinking?'

'You know what I'm thinking,' I said.

And he did. I filled him in.

'The Tyburn is right there,' I said. I pointed across the road to a heavy round iron grid sat in the tarmac of the road like an ancient cowpat.

'You can't, Lee,' he said. 'It can't be that bad. You can't. You've got no kit!'

'You can bring it me,' I replied. 'Not here – it's not safe. I'll make it down to – no, not down . . .' Finn knew as well as I where downstream led to – to Buckingham Palace, to the Parliament buildings – just to more security. 'I'll go up.' I was trying to remember where the easy manholes were. 'Avery Row? Bourdon Place? No, too crowded . . .'

'Way too crowded,' he agreed. Those were all cafe streets like Lansdowne Row. We needed a dipper's street, badly lit, a cul-de-sac . . .

'Stratford Place,' I declared. 'Should be far enough away. Then I can hang out in the old reservoir. It's not that far.' It was further than I wanted to go – but to be honest, so was anywhere – down there.

'It's not safe!' Finn said. 'You've no torch, no waders, no oxygen, nothing . . .'

His face showed right and proper fear of the dreadful world I was about to enter.

'You've got a skello then? Give it me.'

Finn gave me a long, hard look, full of doubt and fear, and then he dredged in his pocket and pulled out a long, hard metal key. I had it off him in a second, and we jumped up and crossed to where the big grid sat. Round the circumference read some worn-down words. I knew it said 'Dudley and Dowell Ltd, Cradley Heath, Staffs' because Dad had taught us that those were the words written on the Tyburn's entrances. I didn't read 'em. But I remembered what they said.

How many people have walked over here, trod on that

manhole cover, and never thought of the little captive river under their feet, still trundling along the same route it had a thousand years ago, running through fields?

We stared down through the little holes of the grid. After a moment our eyes found the distance in the dark, and there, about fifteen feet down, where we knew it would be, black and sparkling like fisherman's glass, gushed the twinkling, filthy waters.

No time to lose. Bruton Lane is quiet but it ain't that quiet. I found the pickhole and within moments I had the heavy iron lid of the manhole levered off. I did not want to hang around, and I did not want him changing his mind and I did not want me changing mine either.

I grinned at him as I slipped down. 'I'm a natural-born tosher, Finn,' I said. 'Ravens can see in the dark, as long as it's the putrid filthy dark of the London shores. It's in my blood. I'll make it up to Stratford Place. Meet me there. Bring some soap and supplies.'

And with that I took my last long breath of the sweet air of West One and slipped down into the undercity world.

My brave face was a complete fake. The shores, the bowels of London for a thousand years, are a hideous and revolting world, a labyrinth full of human excrement and worse. You think I'm exaggerating? A thousand years ago people were already complaining about the stink of them. True, this particular sewer, then, was the nice little River Tyburn flowing from Hampstead down to the Thames, with islands and ducks and pebbles dappling in the sunlight; but for hundreds of years now it's been closed over in a tunnel like a shite-filled route to hell.

Reputable people going down the shores leave the lid off. It can be pretty criking poisonous down there and you want all the fresh air you can get. The flushing gangs – when they still used guys – took oxygen tanks, and a buddy, and a gas mask, and a safety harness, and a radio.

I had nothing. But then I wasn't reputable.

Up above me, calling bye with fear and doubt in his voice, Finn heaved the lid back on, and there I was, suspended in echoey speckled darkness. Perched on the metal rung ladder built into the wall, surveying the pitch darkness of the shores, as Granddad Fred called them, telling his stories of the days when ordure ran in the streets of London and a fellow could make a decent living from toshing for coins and dropped earrings and bits of whatever of this and that that turn up down there – if he could stand the filth (and the miasmas and the gases and the bunnies and the cockroaches and the inspectors' men after you with their lanterns and their guns).

A flurry of activity scuttled past my ear. A bunch of rats or something twitched by and were gone, down in the darkness. Silent again but for the perpetual low roar in the distance, and the gurgles of the Tyburn as it spun along below me.

Like I said, there's three things that Ravens did. We were toshers, flushers or thieves. Nowadays there's no toshing and little quad tractors with CCTV do the flushing, so we've not much choice and that's why I dip for a living. I ain't proud. Seems to me everybody works in ordure one way or another. My family started toshing before the Victorian times, when the sewers were just ditches and gullies covered over, and anyone could reach in and grab a dropped penny if they weren't too dainty. My great-great-great-granddad, whose name was Frederick Bryden Raven, by the end of his life knew the main routes of all the main sewers and most of the local ones: the old ones based on the ditches and the old London rivers that had been covered over as they filled up with filth, and Mr Bazalgette's new ones, which were tall and fine and clean, with steps in and out, and a timetable for the weekly flushings so you could plan to go out the day before and get the week's worth of tosh and not get flushed away. Frederick Bryden had it all in his head, so he could walk from Notting Hill to Whitechapel, from Richmond to Camberwell, upstream and down, all underneath the city and no one would ever know. He made a map of his knowledge of the routes and my dad's still got that map. It's been copied a few times, and things added as explorations were made and changes have come about, but it's still Frederick Bryden's map. I don't know all of it, but I learned a lot when I was a little kid. Billy and Squidge would test me on it. My memory was the best of all of us and when they got on my back about the not-reading business I could floor them with what I remembered.

'Oi, Lee,' they'd say. 'How do you get from Number One Whitechapel and Brick Lane to the King's Scholars' Pond?' And I'd tell 'em you couldn't; you'd have to come up at Holborn because of the sluice gates. That kind of stuff.

Frederick Bryden's son Edward got hepatitis, and there's that rat-piss disease: Weil's disease. Sounds pretty vile too. You'd get bunnies' piss on a cut, then your headache would start, symptoms like flu, and in three days you turn yellow, then you're dead. Well, that's what they say.

Edward's grandson, my granddad Fred, was the one who changed sides. He went and joined the flushers, spending his days scraping shite off the walls, putting it in buckets and winching it up to the real world. I saw a film on the telly once about heart disease and they showed this artery all silted up with fat from junk food and smoking, and it was getting blocked all up so the blood couldn't get through, and the guy was about to have a heart attack from it. There's more fat on the walls of the shores under the West End because of the junk food restaurants, and it goes solid so it's really hard to clean off. Dad told me. And I thought, *What they need is a team of tiny flushers in that guy's arteries, with their brooms and scrapers, cleaning him out, like in the shores.*

All this was in my head while I stood hanging on the metal bars of the staircase, staring down into the darkness. Were these walls going to be slick with fat? Or just sticky and putrid?

I didn't want to go down. All that stuff I told Finn – bravado. All stuff of Dad's that he tried to fill us up with before we knew any better.

Yeah, Dad was a flusher too, for a while. Used it to learn the ropes and the ways. But it was dying by then – technology was coming in instead, all quads and computers and nobody getting their hands dirty. He'd go down freelance though. The shores were extremely bliddy useful to a man in my dad's trade. He didn't actually literally crawl up the sewers into your bathroom, none of us was quite skinny enough for that – though he'd have made me do it if it had been possible, believe me – but he'd take the shores route to the house, and he'd retreat to the shores for the journey home again. The memory of the shores lingered longer in the criminal memory than in the police's, and they seemed to have forgotten that there's another city under the city, with its own roads and alleyways, its main routes and cut-off corners, its bad neighbourhoods, its junctions and its dead ends.

Dad'd taken me down early enough, lying to Mum, and making me lie too. And here I was again. I hitched my hankie up round my mouth and nose with one hand while still holding on to the metal bar of the ladder. The stink was nasty and my membranes were starting to prickle already.

I gave my eyes a few moments to settle, trailed my hand from the ladder to the wall – yeah, greasy – bit my lip and edged my foot into the invisible stream. All I could see of it was glints of daylight freckling this way and that in the dash of blackness. So how would it be for me today?

Oh, Mariani. I should've waited there and got Finn to bring me some waders. There is very little more revolting than wading in shitey water. Wading in watery shite, I suppose. The Tyburn is cleaner than most sewers, with the river water flushing it through all the time. Be thankful . . .

Come on, Lee. It's not that deep. It's not too fast. Small mercies, come on. I filled my mind with images of the clear babbling brook that this was a thousand years ago and started upriver.

I waded midstream. The higher up a sewer you go the smaller it becomes, but I was well downstream here and there was plenty of room even though I was going up. The flow of the river was lively but manageable, and I trailed my hand along the slimy curve of the walls, both to steady myself and to find my way in the dark. The ground beneath me was silty and treacherous, 'to the hazard of my balance and my bones,' as Granddad Fred used to say, but I'd be done with it soon. Sparkling streams Lee, sparkling streams.

Sparkling streams – that's all just crike.

It is horrendous down there. It stinks. It's hot because of all the hotel laundries and restaurants, and there's a steamy shitey smell mixed up with chemical smells and the fat greasy bunnies under your feet . . . any moment my hand could trail across a rat's nest in a hole in the wall. Baby little naked rats.

And the stories don't leave you alone. The herd of pigs that lived up the Fleet sewer, getting fat on eating human effluent. The medical students throwing dead arms and legs in, when they'd finished dissecting them. Murder victims. Dead children. Giant slugs . . . Marauding gangs of thieves. The Fleet exploded once – it was so poisonous and filthy with gases and chemical filth, it just exploded up out of the road, split the street and took three houses with it. It killed some cows, and King's Cross was flooded for days and everyone's houses up there was filled with shite.

Tyburn's not like that though. Tyburn was never as filthy as the Fleet. Really.

I carried on walking. Slow and steady up the incline. It's hard to be steady though when the floor under the filthy mud stream you're wading through is all jagged with broken-up tiling, and invisible holes you could put your foot in and twist it, or break it, and then you'd be done for, rat's piss getting in your blood . . .

I did have a headache. Maybe from all my evil fears.

I snorted a little bitter laugh. It blew up my bandanna and for a moment the warm smell was in my face, naked and revolting. I decided not to laugh again and kept walking.

CHAPTER 5

Continuing the Story According to Mr Maggs

Saturday morning had been unusually busy. That is no excuse. I had been held up late on Friday night by Mr de Saloman, and woken early on Saturday by the girl calling herself Maple, but that is no excuse. I hadn't wanted the book to be left with me in the first place. That is no excuse either. There was no excuse.

Mr de Saloman had consigned his book to my care, and that brat of a horrible boy stole it, and it was my fault. What was I thinking of, leaving him in there alone?

Janaki had gone out to fetch us some lunch when I finally had the opportunity to return to my study after the morning's meetings, which I did specifically with a view to showing Freddy the diary. It was only when I picked up its case that I realized the weight was wrong, which propelled me to look inside, which revealed the sorry truth. The diary was gone.

The only possibility was that the boy had taken it when I placed him in my study earlier that day.

Well, he couldn't have got far. Naturally I called the

police. They told me that they were very busy and would send someone round when they could. I found this attitude rather dismissive, and told them so, and the young man was almost rude to me in response. I couldn't say what I thought it was that I had lost. They would have thought me a mad old man – as perhaps I am.

I much prefer Janaki to make this type of call. She understands modern manners better than I do.

Alas, when Janaki returned, the customary lightening of the heart which I feel on her appearance was soon dashed. Her long hair was awry and her black eyes – always bright – had a glint of fear in them.

'Mr Maggs,' she cried, and her voice was somewhat hoarse, 'sit down. There is bad news.'

'My dear girl,' I said, 'what on earth . . .? Listen, something very bad has happened.'

'Indeed it has,' she replied. 'There has . . .'

And so we continued for a moment, each convinced that our own bad news was worse than the other's, not listening one to the other. In the end, as I am a gentleman, I let her go first.

She read to me from the newspaper.

My face grew longer and more disbelieving with each sentence.

'But that is him – Mr de Saloman!' I cried in a dreadful voice – dreadful even to my own ears.

'I believe it is, Mr Maggs!' she said. 'He – he must have

been killed so soon after leaving here last night! Should we call the police?'

'Janaki, my dear,' I said, 'before you do, hear my tale. The . . . volume . . . that Mr de Saloman left in our care moments before this dreadful fate befell him, for us to keep until his return – it has disappeared. I cannot but think that the boy, this morning, took it.'

I could not bring myself to tell her the nature of the volume that was lost. I wasn't sure and so I could not speak of it.

'What boy? It was a girl,' she said, which confused me.

'What girl?' I replied.

We stared at each other blankly until I remembered the person calling herself Maple who had presented herself practically before dawn.

Could she have taken it? Could she?

'Oh, that girl,' I said.

'Yes, but what boy?' Janaki replied. She's tenacious in these matters.

'The boy who came this morning, while you were in the back.'

She waited a while for me to say something more. Obviously, what I had said was not enough.

'Yes, but what boy was he?' she returned, after a while.

'He was . . .' It was becoming embarrassingly apparent

to me how very foolish I had been. 'He was avoiding some foreign security outside, and seemed to have business with us, so I let him in downstairs.'

'Could he have entered your study though?'

I felt a little warm about the forehead.

'I – er – yes,' I said.

She was just looking at me.

'I admitted him. To my study. And left him there.'

Disbelievingly.

'So he could well have . . .'

Why did you leave a strange security-avoiding boy in your study with a valuable book? I could see the question in her mind, in her thoughts, forming on her lips, but she is a respectful girl, and she did not say it. 'What kind of boy was he?' she said instead.

'Slender, poor-looking, ashy-haired, blue-eyed, prominent upper lip . . .'

'Did he look as if he'd never had a decent meal in his life? Like he was grown in a dark cellar? Sticky-up blonde hair and tattoos on his forearms?'

'Er – yes!' I said.

'I saw him!' she said. 'Not long ago, in the square! He was sitting about under a tree. Come!'

I am not a quick mover, but I did my best. Janaki, with the bounce of youth, was already up the stairs, down the stairs, out the door and on the pavement, running hither and thither like a worried dog, looking for the lad and asking passers-by if they had seen him

A man eating his sandwiches had – heading for Gree▮ Park, he said.

'Come back in and we shall call the police,' I suggested▮ but Janaki pointed out that there were a great many polic▮ already down there as a result of the murder and we shoul▮ just go and address ourselves to them directly.

As I said, Janaki understands modern manners. Withi▮ moments of a policeman saying to her, 'You can't g▮ through here, miss, there's been an incident', we were i▮ a canvas hut talking to a long, bustling woman in a dar▮ suit and several sinister-looking men with curious taste i▮ facial hair and that peculiar little bulge in the neck tha▮ denotes the presence of a subdural communicatio▮ system.

'We believe we know the identity of the dead man,▮ Janaki said.

They stared expectantly.

'He came to visit me last night,' I said sadly. 'He brough▮ a book for me to take care of, and it has been stolen, an▮ he is dead. It is most unfortunate.'

'His name is Ernesto de Saloman,' Janaki continued. 'H▮ was last staying in Paris. He is a bibliophile.'

'The book was stolen by a youth named Joe English,' ▮ said. 'About fourteen, unusually pale, with tattoos. It's a▮ odd manuscript, bound in vellum . . . um . . . possibly ▮ diary of some kind . . .'

'A young girl calling herself Jenny Maple came very early this morning trying to reclaim the book, using a forged letter, but we didn't give it to her.'

The police people stared at us as if in shock. You'd think they'd never been given help with their enquiries before.

CHAPTER 6

Continuing the Story According to Lee Raven

At Stratford Place, just by the Bond Street tube, down underground, there is an old stone room which was a reservoir, they say, from when water was taken from the Tyburn in medieval times and run through a conduit like an aqueduct, all across the city for people to help themselves. On special occasions they'd stop the water and run wine through. They did that for Edward I coming home from the Crusades, and for Henry IV's wedding, and everybody got drunk for free.

It's just sitting there now, under some building behind Oxford Street. It was going to be a museum once, Dad said, but the building's owner wasn't interested. You can still get to it, from the Tyburn, if you're little. Bit of a clamber. I managed to cut my thumb. Not a lot of fun.

That's where I went, to sit and wait for Finn. There was an old ventilation shaft at the front and a drop of yellow light coming down from a grid several levels up. Strange to think that London was down here, then. When you see how the level of the ground has gone up, like when you see ruins and stuff, where does it come from? All that extra earth? Is it a big compost heap? Is it from worms? Is there some network of holes underground, where stuff has been taken from to be spewed up on the surface?

I'm kind of expecting to see old ghosts of monks and drunk peasants and stuff. Dare say Finn'll get up here before dark anyway. The manhole to the surface here is down in the basement area of one of the buildings. Bit public. He'll have to wait till it's safe.

You may be wondering how I know about conduits and monks and stuff, if I can't read and won't go to school. That's because you're making a basic mistake. I ain't stupid. I just can't read. I can learn anything, anywhere, any time. I learned a lot off the telly – history channels and that – and I keep my ears open. So don't go thinking I'm stupid.

One good thing is you don't get hungry down the shores. Food is the last thing on your mind.

I'd taken off my trousers and boots and socks and hung them from the ladder in the neck of the sewer, with the lid back on, so their stink didn't stink me up, and I scraped myself clean as best I could on the stone walls and rubbing myself with gritty dust. The fresh air was beautiful to me. I was standing under the shaft up to the real world and gazing up till my neck ached. I climbed the metal bars up the manhole shaft and felt the cover from beneath, and listened to the heels of the people as they clacked along the pavement way above me, and the rumble and clank of traffic nearby, and they had no idea I was down here.

Finn didn't come.

I knew when the light turned orange and came from a different direction that it was a street light, and it was evening. He'd be along soon. Safer after dark.

He didn't come.

I slept, hunger beginning to sneak in through my dreams, expecting at any moment the rattle of his skello in the pickhole, the clang of the manhole cover. I was half woken when something like a rat ran over my foot, but I can sleep anywhere, I'm good at sleeping.

In the morning it felt like the rats were inside me. Never mind the stink, I was ravenous.

No Finn.

I set myself to think.

I *could* put on my filthy trousers (they might at least be dry by now and I could brush them down), and open the manhole from within with the skello, and take the risk of there being nobody above, and return rather earlier than I had planned to the overworld.

Or I could wait.

What if he didn't have another skello? He'd be able to get one, wouldn't he? Or he'd knock and I'd open it from down here.

I dragged my stiff limbs together and went to peer up the ventilation shaft. The street light was still on, but there was some kind of daylight as well. Dawn. If I was to go, now would be a good time. The West End would be as empty as it would ever be, not that that was any guarantee of any emptiness at all.

I crept up the manhole shaft and listened. For minutes it was quiet. Then trot trot trot trot, someone came clacking by.

I was *hungry*. And thirsty.

I went to the manhole to the sewer and reclaimed my trousers and boots. While there, I took the opportunity for a whazz directly into the hole. One thing at least was convenient.

I decided to wait it out. I didn't want to find myself wandering the West End in daylight, just like I was yesterday only a bit further from the heart of the action and stunk up from being down the shores. I'd stick it out and Finn would come.

It wasn't till mid-morning that it occurred to me to look at the *Beano* book again, to keep myself amused. I'd used it as a pillow the night before, so I went and got it and I took it to the bottom of the ventilation shaft and positioned it and myself in the scrap of light that wavered down, smiled at Plug on the cover, and opened it.

I looked at the Dennis the Menace again first. Then there was some Beryl the Peril, a Little Plum, the Bash Street Kids. I looked at the writing and I didn't mind too much not being able to read it, because there was nobody there telling me I should read it, or I could read it if I tried harder, or I was a stupid useless lump of ignorance for not being able to read it. The letters danced around the way they usually did, and I couldn't really make them out, as I usually couldn't, and it all meant nothing to me. But I loved the pictures, and I could tell what was going on even if I couldn't read the jokes in the speech bubbles. I could half hear my mum's voice from long ago saying, 'And Danny's saying, "Come on, fellows!", and Teacher's saying, "Oh no! Foiled again!"'

I was smiling to myself, curled up with the book, when I realized that I could hear the words. I wasn't remembering them. They were there – in the present.

They weren't just in my head. I could hear them.

I thought: hunger, tiredness, stress. Bad air. Not surprising really. Hearing things. Probably someone up on the street. Voices very peculiar in shafts. Echoes and so on. Could be Finn!

I carefully put the book down and scrambled back up to the manhole. I listened out, silent and alert.

Nothing. A blackbird trilling away, far off. The unmistakable quiet hum of dawn in a big city.

OK.

I came back down to where the book lay, its pages lifting gently in the breath of draught from the ventilations shaft. I picked it up, took it on to my lap and curled myself up again. The shadowy dawn light fell on its pages. I let my eyes settle again on the page, the faded old reds and yellows, the funny faces and knobbly knees, the stupid chases and the silly dogs.

And it started again . . .

There was the voice, in my head or outside it, giving me the words.

Was this what reading was like? Hearing someone else's words in your head? For a moment a pang of envy flew through me like a blade. You could have all that, just by looking at writing . . .

But no – it wasn't that. I wasn't reading. The letters were still blurring and fluttering about, I still couldn't see any of the patterns that I know other people see and make sense of. I wasn't reading. I was hearing. A low, quiet voice, not much louder than my thoughts, was telling me what was written in the speech bubbles. I looked at a bubble and the voice spoke. I looked at another and it spoke again, telling me something else.

I closed my eyes quickly. The voice stopped.

I opened them and looked around. There was no one there. Well, of course there wasn't – I knew that.

I considered looking at the page again.

Maybe not.

I looked.

After a moment, it started again.

It was as if . . . something was reading to me.

It was so lovely. It was the loveliest thing that I had seen or known since . . . since I don't know. It was like having Mum, and a best mate, and me, and all being together and safe, and it was funny . . . it was lovely.

I went through the whole book like that and then I must have dozed off again.

And that was when it got very peculiar.

I went to sleep with an old *Beano Annual* on my lap.

I woke holding on to something else entirely. It was an old book. It was smallish, fattish, and covered in vellum like Mr Maggs had showed me before. Pearly white. Only this had kind of carving in it – etching, you might call it only that probably ain't the right word. It may have looked old but it didn't feel it. It felt kind of flexible; kind of warm in my hands. It wasn't as heavy as it looked either.

I was half asleep. I kind of stared at what I was holding and I blinked, and then I thought, *Oh, I'm still asleep, good dream!* And I did that thing where you try to slip back into sleep because you don't want to lose the dream.

But it wasn't a dream. You don't feel the warmth and the weight in a dream.

So then I sat up, and I looked around a bit, to see if had maybe put the *Beano* somewhere else and this book just happened to be here in my hands all along and I hadn't noticed. But I knew that wasn't the case.

Where the *Beano Annual* had been, right in my hands with Plug on the cover and Mum's Dennis the Menace story inside, there was now an antique tome.

OK.

I didn't know what to say, really. What do you say when something impossible happens before your eyes?

You say, 'There must be an explanation,' that's what you say. And you try to find one.

So I tried to find one.

And all I could think was — even when it was the *Beano*, it was reading aloud to me.

And I stared at this item in my hands and I whispered, 'What the flaming crike are you?'

I dared not be holding it — but it was already there in my hands. I don't know quite how to explain this, but it felt, somehow, kind of like it was alive. Not bouncing around and running away, but — well, if you ever held a baby when it's asleep, or an animal. You know it's not dead. This book was not dead.

I stroked the pearly cover gently. It didn't respond exactly, but . . .

It occurred to me that this item I had nicked was something — how shall I put this? — out of the ordinary. Inconceivable, even. Weird. Magnificent.

Well.

There was only one thing to do. So I did it. I opened the book.

What did I expect? More *Beano* pictures? No. Ancient illuminations in gold and crimson, with mysterious writing in foreign languages? Maybe. Spells to turn my enemies into Surinam toads? Creatures to leap out at me? Magic worlds to draw me in? A beautiful maiden in a strangely realistic picture who turns her face to me with tears in her eyes and soundlessly weeps and begs me to rescue her?

I don't know what I expected. My mouth was dry and I didn't even believe

what had happened so far.

I opened the book.

The pages were blank.

Well – they had nothing written on them, and no pictures. But they were – how can I put this? – they were like the branches of the cherry trees on the streets in March, before the leaves come out in the early spring. You look at them and you can see they're kind of bursting with the leaves they are about to have, the little buds so tight and dark and just about to go . . . BADAAAH! And spring is going to bust out all over with all the blossom and the greenness and everything . . .

That's what these pages looked like. Creamy rough-smooth paper, pulsating with . . .

I touched it. There was a kind of tremor, almost like it was breathing.

'Well, hello,' I said.

The page gave a little ripple under my fingers. And then – the voice again.

'Once upon a time,' it said.

Once upon a time!

I held it up, as if I were reading it, and I gazed at the empty page.

'Once upon a time,' it said gently. The voice was really good. The kind of voice that, whatever it's saying, you turn and listen.

The story was about a little boy called Hercules, who was the strongest child in the world. He held serpents by the neck, their fanged mouths dripping venom . . .

Every now and again one of its pages turned over – not like when they were flapping in the breeze, but as if someone was turning them. But I wasn't. I wouldn't know when to turn.

I breathed slowly, and sat, and listened, and accepted. A book is telling me a story. First it had read me the *Beano*, now it is telling me this. OK.

'The Nemean Lion was born of the Moon,' it continued. 'One furious night she loosed him on to the slopes of Mount Taygetus . . .'

Inside my head, I saw the young lion leaping from the moon, landing on a green and rocky mountainside. It was clearer in my imagination than any cartoon or film. I closed my eyes, and the voice and the words worked magic in me. I could see the lion, smell the warm night, feel the sharpened rock between my fingers as Hercules rose to slay the lion . . .

Hercules was fighting the lion on a Greek hillside when our reverie was shattered.

The clang of the manhole cover came echoing down the shaft. Finn!

The last thing I wanted was to tear myself from the story and the voice. But I had to.

I shook my head back to reality. Well, as best I could. I closed the book swiftly and carefully – 'Sorry,' I whispered – and laid it on my coat to keep it from the dusty floor, covered over with a sleeve. I wasn't ready to explain it, that was for sure. I couldn't have, even if I'd wanted to.

Seeing Finn clambering down the metal ladder filled my heart with normality and joy – and, five minutes later, he'd filled my belly with toasted cheese and salami sandwiches and blueberry yoghurt and chocolate milk and oranges, which was even better.

He had done me proud. A big bag of food, bottles of sherbet and water, clean trousers and a T-shirt, pair of waders, an oxygen puffer, a mask, a torch and a sleeping bag.

'You're going to have to stay here for a while,' he said. 'And I don't know when I'll be able to get back. There's such a fuss you wouldn't believe! You're in the papers again – the police want to talk to you about the dead bloke and parrently you nicked some ancient manuscript off Mr Maggs that belonged to the bloke in the lake – oh, his name is Ernesto de Saloman – and also the Asteriosy thing, but they say you're not to worry about that, they just need to interview you about the murder . . .'

It was rather a lot to take in – especially given my peculiar experiences with the book. But I hadn't lost all my sense. 'Oh yeah,' I said, in disbelieving tones. 'What, they'd let me off dipping Asteriosy if I just put myself in their hands long enough to say I don't know bog all about Mr Ernesto and here's your book, I never wanted it anyway?'

'That's what they're saying,' said Finn.

'Yeah, well, Ravens don't go to the police,' I continued. 'And even if the police did mean it – fat chance – I don't suppose Romana Asteriosy's security would think of things that way . . .'

And anyway . . . the book. I may have not been that interested in the book before, but that was before . . .

'You should think about it,' said Finn, reasonable as ever. And maybe if I'd been a sensible person, clear-headed and not in a state of shock from having a book read him stories about lions being born of the moon, I would've gone up and handed myself in, and got my botty smacked and helped clear up the murder just by letting them know it was nothing to do with me and they needed to look else-where. And then, let's imagine, best possible scenario, they'd be so pleased I'd helped them they'd protect me from Mrs Asteriosy . . . as if . . . and even so, no. It all led to trouble, and back to Mum and Dad and school. I wasn't going back.

Crike. Dad would have seen it if I was in the papers.

He'd know where I'd hide! He'd taught me everything I know! He'd use the same logic I used and track me down in no time.

He wouldn't go to the police, that's for sure. Ravens don't go to the police.

He might come down here though. Mariani! I'd have to move on.

'I ran into Billy,' said Finn.

That's all I need.

'And?' I said. I had to concentrate on this stuff. Never mind the book for a moment. Pin your mind to what Finn's telling you.

'He'd seen about it. Wanted to know had I seen you, and it was hard, Lee – I told him I hadn't though. He'll slaughter me when he finds out. Anyway he said it's lucky Dad's away, he's gone to Paris on some job, but he'll be back next weekend.'

By my reckoning today was Sunday. A lot could happen in a week.

'And . . . er . . .' Finn was trying to say something. 'I brought the papers. I . . . er . . . I could read 'em to you . . .'

It was understandable that he should be reluctant to offer. I've clocked people for trying to help me that way before now. But not Finn. Finn's not like that. Anyway, I needed to know what was going on.

This is what Finn read:

CORPSE IN LAKE
IDENTIFIED
BUT MYSTERY DEEPENS
Reward offered for information
Where is the missing manuscript?

The mysterious corpse found in Rosamund's Pond, Green Park, in the small hours of Saturday morning has been identified as Ernesto de Saloman, 49, a French businessman who had been staying at the Ritz Hotel on nearby Piccadilly. Mr de Saloman, a father of three, originally from Marseilles, was believed to have been in London on business. He was last seen alive late on Friday evening when he visited the antiquarian bookseller Edward Maggs at his emporium in Berkeley Square.

Police revealed that Mr de Saloman had left a book in Mr Maggs's care which has since been stolen by a visitor to the premises. The manuscript, described by the police as 'white leather' and 'old-looking', is said to contain ancient legends in French. Police are looking for a youth named as Joe English, described as aged 13–15, about five feet six inches tall, of slender build, with noticeably blonde hair and tattooed forearms.

They also wish to interview a young girl seen in the vicinity early on Saturday morning, described as about 14 years old, around five feet four inches, with brown hair and a healthy complexion, wearing a cloak and named as Jenny Maple. Anyone having information about either of these two individuals is asked to contact the police witness line on 020 7010 3000.

The famous children's author Nigella Lurch has offered a reward of 25,000 dirhams for the recovery of the manuscript. In a statement issued by her publishers, she said, 'Ernesto de Saloman was a good man and a good friend of mine. I am deeply upset at his dreadful fate and my heart goes out to his wife and family at this difficult time. The loss of this precious manuscript — which he had in fact recently given to me as a gift — only adds insult to injury.' Ms Lurch is the author of the Cotton MacGill Mysteries, which were very successful some years ago.

A further note of mystery remains. An unnamed source apparently heard a man's voice crying out the name 'Elly-Anne' and some words of French at around two a.m.

When he'd finished Finn looked up at me. 'So did you nick that manuscript then? Have you got it?'

'No,' I lied automatically. My head was reeling. It wasn't just the great amount of trouble I was in, or the ever-larger number of people I was in trouble with. Now there was caio involved!

Twenty-five thousand dirhams is a load of money.

I don't want anybody thinking I've got anything worth that much on me. It ain't safe.

Twenty-five thousand dirhams! If I played my cards right, I could get that. Me! Stupid Lee!

'Pity,' said Finn, ''cos if you did have, obviously you wouldn't be able to take it back and get the reward what with they think you're the thief, so you'd need someone you trust, like, you know, your brother or something, who could take it for you and then you'd be really rich. And you'd give them a cut of course.' He looked at me with a hopeful expression, bug-eyed, like a frog with ideas.

'Yeah,' I said. 'Well, if I had it, I'd probably do just that.'

But I did have it, and I wasn't doing that.

Why not?

Twenty-five thousand dirhams!

I was going to have to have a think. Twenty-five thousand dirhams could change a boy's life.

Finn went soon enough after that. I was left alone with a couple of questions burning.

What in crike *was* this book?

And how exactly did I feel about 25,000 dirhams?

Well, looked like I'd have plenty of time to find out.

I unfolded it from its hiding place and took it back to our cosy little spot under the ventilation shaft.

'OK, Hercules!' I said cheerfully. 'Let's see!'

Half of me thought it wouldn't happen again. Seeing Finn had brought me back to reality. I must have been hallucinating. It happens. There's weird things in the air down the shores.

Well, soon as we sat down, soon as I opened the book, the story started again. I didn't even have to look at the page. I shook my head in relief and disbelief, and after a while I settled myself on my back on the floor, holding the book next to my heart, and let the story sweep me away.

I lay there all day.

The cold seeped into my back. My legs grew stiff. My mind and my heart filled up with the story. I was really really happy. Even after Hercules finished his twelve labours, I just lay there with a stupid grin on my face. Happy. Going over the story in my mind. Hercules was like a flusher, cleaning out that filthy stable! I was happy.

It was so quiet that a little mouse ran over the book as it lay warm on my chest. Then another! I just flicked at them with my hand.

After about half an hour of this quiet happiness, I heard the voice again.

'Excuse me,' it said.

Another story! Great beginning. I thought about sitting up, to encourage it, but decided against. As if my behaviour would affect what it did! Either it was some miraculous piece of kit, some bit of electronica from a richer world than I've ever seen, some top-of-the-range antique-styled info-pod, or it was – well, a miracle. A magic thing. Either way – and to be honest I knew it wasn't an info-pod – it would hardly care about me.

It gave a small cough.

Now that confused me. I know a story could start with "'Excuse me'" – followed perhaps by 'sneered the fat man, stroking the white cat, but I think you are under some misapprehension . . .'; or 'squawked the Duchess, and Murdoch the Wonderthief knew immediately that the game was up . . .'; or . . . Well, anyway, it could, but I didn't see how any story could begin 'Excuse me' followed by a small cough. I don't suppose anybody knows how to spell a small cough. They'd write, 'The Duchess gave a small cough' – wouldn't they? I don't know a lot about writing, obviously, but it seems . . .

Anyway, then it coughed again and said, 'Um, do you want another story?'

And that certainly wasn't the beginning of a story. That was an invitation. An offer.

That was conversation.

It said, 'Because if you do, that's fine, but if you don't, would you mind closing me?'

I sat up quickly. A bit too quickly. The book fell from my chest to the floor.

It said, 'Ouch.'

And then I swore. Quite a lot.

And it said, 'Gosh.' Like some vicar in an old film.

'Sorry,' I said.

'No,' it replied, 'not at all. I'm filled with admiration. That's some vocabulary. Could you pick me up?'

And I thought, *I'm talking to a book and book is talking to me.*

There must be something very strong in the sewers of Soho tonight. Maybe all the pee from all the nightclubs is full of drugs . . . Maybe . . .

But it felt so real.

I picked it up. Brushed it off gently.

'Thank you,' it said.

My mouth fell open, but I didn't swear again.

CHAPTER 7

The Story According to the Book

I did not mean to speak to the boy. Not even to tell him a story. I know I gave him the fright of his life – I've done that many many times before – but really, what was I meant to do? Giving them stories is my job. It has been for thousands of years. So if he can't read, what am I meant to do? And then he leaves me lying open right over his story-hungry heart? I had no choice. I had to get round it somehow.

And odd as it may seem, I've never really met an illiterate person before. You'd think I would have, over time, but all this time, I've always been in libraries and monasteries and so on – not by choice – you think I get any choice where I go? You try being a book. You go where you're put, and that's it . . . Where was I? Oh yes, and when I *was* out in the world, in the old days, I was in Mesopotamia and everyone could read then.

When his brother had left, and he turned and picked me up again, he had a question burning in his blood and I felt it. I felt it as strongly as I had felt his inability to read, when he had rested his head on me the night before I had to answer it.

It was a joy to tell him of the Labours of Hercules, lying on his heart. I could feel his pulse race at the exciting bits, hear his held breath at the suspense, his relief when things went right.

But then, when he left me open, for half an hour . . . well, he couldn't know it, but when I am open I have to tell a story. Usually I just have it in place in writing, and can wait for someone to come and read. But lying there on his heart, having been speaking – speaking! – the compulsion was so strong, the link so close . . . But I couldn't tell a story till he turned back to the beginning.

I couldn't keep it in. I was going to burst. So I asked him.

I thought he took it rather well.

After the swearing, I asked him again, very gently, and still in shock I think, he nodded.

He settled himself back down on the floor in that rather dark undergroundy place – I hoped we weren't going to stay there too long – and turned to the beginning.

'Would you like the story of me?' I asked him.

'Oh yes,' he murmured.

Of course he would. I like to give people what they want.

'Many thousands of years ago,' I began, 'there was a young god called Nebo. He had fine dark eyes and a curly beard. He was young and handsome and extremely clever, and he rode on a winged dragon called Mushusshu, who really belonged to his father, Marduk, but Nebo was allowed to use her whenever he wanted and after a while he just took her over, because his father preferred his chariot and never took her out. Mushusshu was not the cleverest dragon in the world but she was extremely loyal and she had lots and lots of babies, whom Nebo loved very much. They were extremely sweet, actually. All different colours, sparkly and gleaming. There was one very dear one called Squabo, who played such tricks . . . Well, previously Nebo had been in Sumeria, where he had been a woman, but it was when he went to Babylon, to his city of Borsippa, that he came into his strength and the great days of his existence, and this is how it happened.

'One day Nebo was out walking by the River Tigris in the Garden of Eden, and he saw his father down on the river bank. The river is wide and beautiful there, the land flat and green around it, with palm trees and rushes growing, and smooth red mud in the curves along the banks. (At least it was like that then. It may be very different now.) Marduk (he has plenty of other names, but we'll stick with Marduk for simplicity) was standing there, on the grass, looking around. He had only recently made the world, separating off the light from the dark, and the heavens from the earth, and the earth from the waters, and he was taking a rest, admiring what he had made – how clean and beautiful it was, so colourful and clear and imaginative, and full of details. Now he was thinking about making living things for his beautiful new world, to live in it.

'*I could have ones that creep about on the ground,* Marduk thought, *and ones to swim in the river, and really pretty ones to fly in the air and catch the light on their wings . . . and I'll make one that looks like me, to give them names and look after them all . . .*

'First he made a little manikin: he took a lump of clay from the river bank and squidged it in his fingers to give it arms and legs and a head, with a tuft of reed fronds for hair, and a little face. It looked cute.

'"That's nice," said Nebo. "What is it?"

'"Man," said Marduk. "It's only a prototype. The real thing should be bigger." And he carved out a big pile of squidgy red clay from the river bank, about as big as a man. Then he worked in the warm sunlight of only the sixth day of the world's existence, with a sweet gentle breeze coming off the river, and the swishing green reeds singing to him, and he started to make a model of himself. He was on his knees for much of the work, leaning over it like you do when you make a sandcastle, balancing himself on one arm, getting red streaks on his robe, smiling to himself as it took shape. Two good legs, two strong arms, a head and a torso . . .

'"What shall I call him?" he said after a while.

'Nebo, squatting down nearby and watching the work, said, "How about Red Earth, after what he's made of?" Red Earth in their language is *adam* – so that's what he was named.

'Marduk had made Adam's chest too broad, so he scraped it down with a sharp stone (a stick might have been better but there were no sticks because no branches had fallen off any trees yet). He squished the extra bits of clay into a lump and dropped them on the vivid new green grass by his side.

'"Is he ready?" asked Marduk.

'"Looks good from here," said Nebo.

'So Marduk leaned forward and breathed life into his first man.

'"Ahhh," said Nebo.

'"What do you think?" Marduk asked.

'"Nice," said Nebo. He picked up a bit of the discarded clay. "Can I have a bit?"

'"Of course," said Marduk. "Careful what you do with it though. I breathed on that bit too."'

I paused for a moment. The boy was lying still, happy, interested.

'That was me,' I said, pausing for effect. But then: 'What do you mean,' asked the boy, 'that was you?'

I was rather surprised at this.

'Young man!' I said sternly. 'When humans read you, they cannot interrupt. Please!'

'They can close you and put you down,' he said.

'Yes, I know . . .'

'They can fall asleep while they're reading and leave you in the middle of a sentence.'

'Yes, they can, though I do wish they wouldn't . . .'

'And they can let you slip from their fingers and fall on the floor.'

'Yes, yes, all right . . .'

'And they often have questions, I bet.'

Now that hadn't occurred to me.

'Do you think so?'

'Sure – like when they look things up in the back and they're not there and they get narked.'

'Ah,' I said.

'So, what do you mean about being the lump of mud?'

'Hush,' I replied. 'All in good time.'

'But you're not a lump of mud. A book ain't a lump of mud.'

'Shh,' I said. 'Patience. All will be revealed. All right?' And I continued.

'That evening, Nebo sat in his courtyard, with his lantern twinkling in the dusk like a firefly, washing me in cool water, removing the odd worm – that was Marduk's mistake, he left the worms in Adam – and bits of grass and so on that I had picked up down by the river. Then he left for me a day or two to dry out. I came to on a stone slab in his courtyard, out of the sun, and with a jar of water to keep me soft, and he began to slap me about and shape me. (I didn't mind – it was what I was for). He flattened me and he smoothed me down and he rinsed me off, and then he took a sharp little blade and he stuck it into me. Over and over.'

'What he want to do that for?' exclaimed Lee. 'That's not very nice.'

'It's what I was for,' I said. 'Listen, and you shall learn. He was inventing writing. On me! He stuck the blade into me, leaving a little shape like an arrowhead. He made them large and then small. He made them in groups, in patterns. He made patterns for numbers: simple. He made patterns for goats and chickens. He made collections of patterns, lines like stars and specks and arrowheads and arrowtails. He made patterns for money. He made the names of gods. He wrote about what his father had done by the river, creating man. Then, before I dried out, he smoothed me again and rinsed me down and rekneaded me and started again.

'And he gave writing to mankind. This is why he was so loved, so honoured and worshipped. For what good is all the knowledge in the world if it isn't written down? Nebo gave mankind the means to remember everything they ever learned, and to pass their knowledge down through the generations, and to build upon the knowledge that had come down to them. Without him, mankind would still be living in holes.

'And he gave them stories as well. He made a long long

pattern, a story about somebody called Gilgamesh, how he was set up against a man called Eabo, the adventures they had together. There was a monster in the forest, a great voyage, a wise man. The friend died. He had to go to a great lake under the earth, where all the dead people hung around. Gilgamesh, who was still alive, went after him, to find out what had happened, and how he could escape death.'

'Do you still know that story?' asked the boy.

'I know all stories,' I replied. 'That was a good story, and it was the first, but there have been better ones since.'

'Um . . . Can I ask you something?' he said.

'I do wish you'd stop interrupting,' I said. 'How are we going to get anywhere if you keep interrupting?'

'Are you telling me a story? Or are you talking to me?'

'Well, I'm trying to tell you a story . . .'

'Because, you see, I had just about started to think I might be able to get my head around the idea of a book telling me a story out loud, and now it looks like this is more of a conversation, know what I mean?'

'Yes, I know what you mean by the word conversation. I am, after all, a book.'

'Yeah but . . .' he said.

'Yeah but what?' I replied, patiently I thought.

'Yeah but you're chatting away —'

'Well, yes . . .'

'And I had just thought, well, maybe you were like some kind of MP9 player or something, you know, a fancy one, but now . . . I don't know what you are.'

'I'm a book,' I said. 'I would have thought that was quite obvious.'

'Yeah but . . .'

'Yeah but what?'

'We're having a chat. It's not usual, is it?'

I had to concede that indeed it wasn't usual.

'I'm talking to a thing,' he said, with an air of metaphysical puzzlement.

'Less of that, if you don't mind,' I said. 'I may be a thing, but you don't need to say so.'

'Do you talk to everybody?' he asked.

'Well, no,' I said.

'Did you talk to Mr Maggs?'

'Of course not. There was no need,' I replied.

He didn't need to ask why I *did* need to talk to *him*. He knew he couldn't read.

He was quiet for a moment. Then: 'Are you magic?' he said suddenly.

'I was telling you what I am,' I said mildly. 'Before I was interrupted.'

Oh,' he said. 'Sorry. Carry on.'

So I carried on.

'Nebo lived in his temple at Borsippa. Every New Year

he was carried out in style to visit his father across the river at Babylon. He was given a beautiful and clever wife, Tashmet, who helped him in all his projects and was as beloved as he. He was known as the Prophet, the Proclaimer, the Teacher, the Hearer, Nizu – the God Who Knows, All-Wise, All-Knowing, Dim Sara – Creator of the Writing of the Scribes, the Mighty Son, the Director of the Whole of Heaven and Earth, Holder of the Tablet, Bearer of the Writing Reed of the Tablet of Destiny, Lengthener of Days, Vivifier of the Dead, Stabilizer of Light for Men who are Troubled . . . well, he was known as all sorts of things and he was god of astrology and wisdom, agriculture, schools, reading and writing. All sorts of useful things.

'And I lived with him, and he wrote on me. I loved the feeling of being written on. It was as if something already in me was being released. And I stayed a long time in Nebo's courtyard. He created the first library: more and more clay was brought, and divided into lumps, and smoothed into tablets, and scratched on, and dried.

'But I was not like the others. I was special. Nebo kept using me over and over. I never dried out. I was alive! I would lie in the shade, and I never got baked, and he became fond of me. He would try things out on me and then have them copied tidily on to other tablets. Sometimes at night, when the yellow moon rose high and the night-ingales sang down by the river, when Nebo would retire to his platform to sleep, he would take me with him, so he could write down his dreams when he woke in the night . . .

'I was the tablet he held. I was the Tablet of Destiny.

'And all the time I sensed, all around me, the rush and flurry of the human beings. I especially liked the small ones – the babies who gasped in amazement at their own fingers and toes, the tiny ones who were beginning to notice things outside of themselves. Most of all I liked the bigger ones who were beginning to learn how to think.

'And, bit by bit, they began to wonder about love and death, and sex and truth. And for every stage, the stories Nebo had scratched were there to guide them through.'

I paused, rather pleased with my turn of phrase.

And that blighter boy interrupted again.

'So how come you're a book?' he asked. 'And how come you were the *Beano*? How come you can talk? And how come you were blank? And how come in the paper they said you were myths from Mesopotamia? In French?'

'Boy!' I said. 'Little boy! I am from the clay which made man! The god who breathed life into Adam breathed life into me! The god who created writing, created it on me! I can do . . . many things.'

He was silent.

I could feel his confusion and puzzlement.

'Dude!' he cried. 'That is . . . But . . .'

'Of course you don't understand,' I said kindly. 'It is a great mystery and has been baffling humans for a long long time. I wouldn't worry about it if I were you, but of course you will worry about it whatever I say . . . You look puzzled.'

I paused.

And he replied, 'How do you know?' Not in a cheeky way. 'Can you see me?' he said.

'Yes,' I said.

'How?' he asked keenly. 'Have you got eyes?'

'In a way,' I said cautiously.

'Have you got a brain? It said in *Harry Potter* never trust anything if you can't see where it keeps its brain. Where would you keep your brain?'

Well.

As I had never talked to a human before, I hadn't any experience of what wonderful and absurd questions they might ask. Of course the boy was just awash with curiosity.

'My brain is of the spirit,' I said. 'So are my eyes.'

'Yer what?' he said.

'The spirit,' I said. 'Like – like a ghost. Can a ghost see?'

'Course,' said the boy.

'Do you know where a ghost keeps its brain?'

'It keeps its ghosty brain in its ghosty head, but anyway I don't trust a ghost.'

'Don't you trust me?'

'I –' He thought for a moment. 'I trust you a lot, but

I don't know what you are and I'm talking to a book and it's just possible I've lost my marbles, or you're, I dunno, some big trick. I'd like to know what you are.'

'I told you,' I said. 'I was telling you.'

'Sorry,' he said. 'Carry on. It's just . . .'

'What?'

'I'd like to see your face.'

Well, that took me by surprise. My face!

Never underestimate a human . . .

'Well, that might be a bit difficult,' I said. 'Now may I continue?'

But he wouldn't let it go.

'Have you got a face?' he asked. He was staring at me, rather desperately, as if trying to find a face that he could read and communicate with, a face with warmth and expressions, and eyes revealing the thoughts, and a mouth to smile and a nose to wrinkle, cheeks to crease up with laughter . . . For human communication the words alone are not enough.

'Yes, I have a face,' I admitted. Now why did I tell him that?

'Where is it?' he said. 'Where do you keep it?'

'Hidden,' I said, and my tone of voice let him know it was to remain so. 'Now. Where were we . . .? Ah yes. Mesopotamia. Nebo spent much time at his great temple at Nineveh. I lived there in the special book-room, in a jar. We were all tidily arranged and catalogued. It was a very pleasant place. The Babylonians and the Assyrians were very organized about libraries, you know. People could come and borrow us. Each tablet had a little tag on it saying what book it was part of, and what number it was, with a curse for bringing it back late. We'd just sit in our jars, waiting . . .'

I went off in a little dream of the happy quiet days in the library at Nineveh.

I was pulled back by the boy's voice.

'And what happened?'

'The palace was burned,' I said. 'The temple was razed to the ground and the library was scattered.' I could hear the bitterness entering my voice. This was part of the story I did not like to linger on – the first I saw of the worms in human nature, of war and violence and hatred. I gathered myself, and continued: 'Nebo, after some centuries, moved to Egypt, where he lived as the bird-headed Thoth. Those were good years . . . He weighed the hearts of men against the feather of truth at their death, and wrote their judgement . . . In Greece too he was loved. They called him Hermes. In Rome they named him Mercury, and put Mushusshu's wings on his heels and his helmet. Later, he was required to retreat from the world of men. Rival gods grew up. Judaism and later Christianity . . . He was no longer loved and respected, and the world of men was no longer a safe place for him.' I paused. 'I – meanwhile – due to an oversight – had been borrowed, and the oaf never took me back. He wrote a list on my back of what he was shipping to Memphis – phials of different qualities of oil of roses, if I remember – and gave me to the captain of the felucca –'

'What's a felucca?'

'A boat on the Nile – anyway, I fell in. Plop. And sank. The cool water rushed up over me and enveloped me, and for months I just lay, mingling with mud and watching the pale bellies of the Nile perch swim up and swim down above me, and the reeds blow this way and that, and the pink granite glow beneath the surface of the clear water when the angle of the sun was right, and the lines of the fishermen come down, and rise up, sometimes with a Nile perch on them and sometimes without. Sometimes at night when the water was still and glassy I could see the moon, high up above me, through the water and the night, and I remembered Nebo's platform by the Tigris and how useful I had been, and how he loved me . . . I thought I would just wash away altogether . . .

'But one day the river was hugely changed – a great movement came upon it, a flowing and flooding and lurching of water, cloudiness and cold washing through, and all the fishes panicked, and the reeds clutched their patch of mud, and the birds flew up in tatters of fear and the water spread out across the land, so that flowers bloomed underwater like the faces of drowned maidens, and their leaves trailed behind them like their drowned hair. It was the annual great inundation, when the Nile floods the surrounding lands. The mud became water and water became mud, and I was spread across a field of warm swamp, and I settled into a new life around the roots of a papyrus patch.

'And the next thing I knew was I was green and feathery and waving in the wind, solid and fresh and reaching for the sun, hot and happy. I was like that for many months of the spring and summer, and I enjoyed it very much. I loved to watch the beautiful white egrets, swinging like clean laundry in the acacia trees, and some of them were foolish enough to try and sit on me, which was funny.

'And then one bright and beautiful morning in the fullness of my feathery days, I was sliced down, and slit open, and my innards were scraped from me with a sharp knife and I was dried out, spread flat, layered and kippered, and cut and trimmed and put out for sale as several fine pages of Hieratica parchment, top quality, very white and clean, much favoured by priests. My trimmings were used for Emporetica – wrapping paper. I lost touch with them.

'And what did those Egyptian priests do with me? They pasted me together till I was fifty metres long, wrote *The Book of the Dead* on me, rolled me up and stuck me in with a mummy for the rest of eternity . . .'

The boy had been staring in gratifying amazement, but at this he found his voice again. 'What was that like?' he whispered. 'I've seen mummies. When I was at school we went to the British Museum . . .'

I knew what he was thinking. He was thinking of real dried-up dead people, and their coffins all covered in curses.

'Dark,' I told him. 'Not lonely, because the tombs were full of magic things. There was a very nice canopic jar which became a particular friend, and the heart scarabs were always sweet – they always chose the gentlest ones for the job. And my darling mice, of course . . . but the murmurings got a bit much. You know, all I wanted really was light, and air, and life, and people to read me so I could tell them all the stories I know . . .'

'You probably don't like being down here then,' said Lee. 'In the dark, and underground again, and all . . .'

'Well, I don't mind,' I said. And then I rather surprised myself. I found myself saying, 'It's nice having you here. You're interesting – you see . . .'

I hesitated a moment.

'What?' said the boy.

'This may sound strange,' I said, 'especially considering how many many centuries, indeed millennia, I have existed, and how many peasants and slaves and illiterates must have passed by me, but I've never really met an illiterate person before . . . not close up. Because of always being with priests, and in libraries. And in Babylon everybody learned to read and write . . . I've never had to deal with someone who can't read me.'

The boy, I could see, didn't know whether to feel big or small.

'Oh,' he said.

'It's quite nice,' I said. 'I like that you're interested in me even though you can't read me.'

'Oh,' said Lee again. 'Well – of course I am. Real books are no use to me. But you're different.'

'Thank you,' I said.

'Well, thank you,' he said, and we sat there in silence for a moment. I think we were both a little embarrassed.

'And thank you for being the *Beano*,' he said. 'I liked that.'

'You're welcome.'

What a funny mixture of boy he was! So brave and tough, and yet so sad; a thief, a desperado, but with a heart that left to itself would be as pure as a young stream.

'Um,' said the boy, after a while.

'What, my dear fellow?' I answered.

'If we're to have conversations, I think I ought to know your name. We should introduce ourselves.'

'Well, you're Lee,' I said.

'How do you know that?' he asked.

'Because I know things,' I said. I wasn't going to tell him how I know what I know. It's just there. I catch it, somehow. Or perhaps it was there all along. I've had a long time to think about it, and I think that what I have is the ability to catch everything from the humans and not forget it. I'm sure the stories start from the humans, not from me. Certain. How I catch their thoughts and stories and knowledge, I don't know. But I do.

'So what do I call you?' he enquired. 'Tablet of Destiny seems a little formal, but if you like . . .'

'Well, I'm most often known as the Book of Nebo nowadays,' I said.

'Bit of a mouthful,' he observed. 'What do your friends call you?'

Had I eyes, I would have shot him a look. I just sighed in a very slightly exasperated fashion.

'Well,' I said, 'there hasn't really been any occasion in the past 12,000 years for anybody to address me by name.'

'Really?' he said. 'But . . .'

I just waited for it to sink in.

Finally he exclaimed, 'What – but – have you never talked to anybody else?'

'No,' I said.

'For 12,000 years?'

'Yes.'

'So I'm the first?'

'Yes,' I said.

'But that's – that's amazing – that's completely bliddy –'
He was really really pleased.

'Yes,' I said.

'First person a book like you ever talks to is me! Little old Lee, who can't even read! Ha ha ha!'

His laughter was a delightful sound. After a bit it subsided.

'So what would you like me to call you?' he asked.

'I don't know,' I said.

'I could just call you Nebo,' he suggested.

'Oh no, no, no,' I said quickly. 'I don't think so. We'll think of a name for me. Later. But now you'll be getting tired. I'll tell you more tomorrow.'

I could see he was peeved.

Ah well. Make 'em laugh, make 'em cry, make 'em wait, as one great story-teller said.

CHAPTER 8

The Story According to Nigella Lurch

My father was a writer, you know. A wonderful writer. Throughout my childhood he would write and write and write and write. I was not allowed to disturb him, of course. His writing was too important. Whenever I rested my head against his study door I would hear him tapping away behind it on his computer. I would sit there for long hours, thinking about how hard he worked and what a great writer he was.

When he came out he was very kind to me. But he didn't come out that much.

'Don't disturb your father, he's writing,' my mother would say. When I was very young she would say it sweetly, with an air of excitement. As I grew older the tone gradually changed. I learned to associate the new tone with the fact that although he wrote all the time, there were no books. He was a writer, but he was unpublished. No publisher was bright enough to see how talented he was. It was the great bitterness of his life, and my mother's. It was a blight on our family.

Well. When I was quite young, we were staying in Cairo.

He had taken a job – his first – and everyone was ashamed by it, because great writers should not have to take jobs in museums in Cairo. This was where I first heard of the book. Of course I thought it was nonsense.

My mother was unhappy. My father was aware of this and shamed by his inability to give her lots of money and a glamorous life. The apartment was too hot, too grubby. There were too many other people. She took rooms instead in a rich-world hotel out by the pyramids, where she could remain cool. Her father paid for it.

My father was working hard, at the museum, and in the evenings writing his novel which was going to change the world. He suggested my mother and I take a trip up the Nile.

'Temples,' he suggested. 'Tombs. Palms. Hippopotamuses!'

My mother yawned.

'Camels! And crocodiles!' he said, with a cheerful glance at me.

I smiled back at him. It was so lovely to have him chatting with us.

'A clean, modern white ship with a shady deck, running water, good fresh food, a river breeze,' he said, and started humming a little Arab tune that sounded like the wind. He very much wanted to please my mother. She looked up. She liked to lie in the sun, reading romances and showing off her legs.

'A rich-world boat?' she asked.

'I was thinking about a small boat, a small party . . .'

Not up my mother's street at all. I knew that some people liked to go slumming into what they called 'reality', but not my mother.

'Oh, lord, no,' said my mother. 'I should be bored to sobs. Find a nice ship with some fun people. You know. My kind of people. Cocktails? Cards?'

So I found myself on a large shining ship cruising the Nile, having my cheeks pinched by gin-drinking old women, and being sent to bed every night at seven so that my mother had more time to try on all her dresses and powder her nose. In order to annoy her, I pretended to mind very much that I was hardly allowed to visit any of the temples and tombs. In truth I was not at all bothered. Mummies and sphinxes and bird-headed gods from thousands of years ago meant nothing to me. I had seen pictures of these things. Why should I bother to leave the cool and airy ship and go out in the flaming African sun? If my father had been with me to show me it might have been different.

The only person who was at all kind to me was a young lieutenant, John Matthews. I spent most of my time reading, and I had some schoolwork I was meant to complete before our trip was over, so he showed me the small library on the ship, where I was able to inveigle him into going on the Internet, getting me all the information

I needed and writing a lot of it up for me. He also tried to interest me in stories and tales of ancient Egypt, and it was he who told me of the legendary *Book of Nebo*, in which all stories are written.

It was a particularly hot afternoon and I decided to torment him for my amusement.

'How could all stories be written in one book? No book could be big enough.'

'Aha,' he said, in the annoying tone of one who thinks he knows better. 'They are not all in there at once.'

Pathetic. I could knock that down easily. 'Then they're not in there, are they? If they're not in there . . .' I said it in an irritating singsong way.

'They appear when they are needed,' he said.

'What, by magic?' I sneered.

'By some mysterious means, yes,' he said. 'The book has a different story in it each time you read it.'

'So if you put it down at night and want to finish the story the next day, you can't,' I said. 'Very nice.'

'I think it lets you finish the story you're reading, but when you go back to the beginning, it's a new story.'

'So how could it be every story ever told? Half of them haven't been told yet. So if it was the book of this old god, Nebo, how could they have stories from now? Or any of the stories between then and now?' I'm afraid I rather liked to make grown-ups look stupid.

'I don't know, Nigella. But I would think if a book were

magic and mysterious enough to have a new story in it every time someone turned to its opening page, it could probably manage a little thing like time pretty easily.' He smiled at me in a way I didn't like – a wise, avuncular, friendly smile, patient and fond. I wished he wouldn't.

I was annoyed and went away to kick things on deck. That was too hot, so I decided to be ill, so that my mother would have to make somebody bring me something cold to drink. I returned to our cabin and started to throw up, and rang the bell, and required the steward to fetch my mother.

Before she arrived I changed my mind. I would not be ill – I would do something even more annoying.

'Mother,' I said, 'it's not good for me being stuck on the ship. Why can't we go ashore? There's all that interesting culture to see, and those trips the others go on. There's one this evening. Can't we go to the temple, Mother? And see the things? I'd love to learn about the ancient Egyptians.'

She was furious. The grown-ups on the boat had divided into the people who went ashore and the people who sat about laughing and drinking. My mother was naturally among the latter. She wanted to have a cool shower and put on another pretty dress and drink more cocktails and smoke and let her laughter drift across the deck out over the still waters of the river. She wanted to play cards, and make some man go and fetch her wrap when it grew chilly.

'Father will ask me what I saw when we get back to Cairo,' I said plaintively. 'And I don't want to tell him I saw nothing. Please. Mother, please!'

The mention of my father was very clever of me. I knew it would get to her, because it was true.

For a moment her face was suffused with anger and then, just like that, she switched it to a charming smile and said, 'Of course, darling! We've been far too engrossed with all this fun on board. We'll go ashore tonight, just you and I, and we'll have a lovely lovely time.'

She often talked like that, like someone out of an old film. It was stupid.

Of course it wasn't just she and I. It was she, I, all the others who usually went on the shore trips – the Shore Bores, she called them – and John Matthews, who knew them all and chatted with the guide and seemed genuinely interested in the things we were shown.

Tonight it was indeed a temple. I can't remember what it was called, but we had to go by bus and there were all these donkeys and poor-world people outside and it was pretty scuzzy, but when we got there there was a nice big air-conditioned visitors' centre with a bar for tourists only, so that was all right. My mother couldn't bear having poor-world people come up to her and I have to say I shared her view. They were really weird-looking. None of the women had make-up or facelifts or anything, and the children had no shoes.

Anyway, the temple was OK – I don't know why they were so proud of that stuff, it was much smaller than what we build now, and a lot of it had fallen down or been knocked about by other people from hundreds of years ago. Really, who cared? But there were some quite good carvings on the wall of someone holding about eight enemies by the hair and bashing them. 'Smiting', the guide said. The guide was this pretty black woman, and she knew how to read the hieroglyphics, which was all the little pictures and things carved on the wall. Matthews really liked her and for some reason he wanted me to as well. He kept calling me over and trying to be interesting.

At one point he called, 'Hey, Nigella – look, this is about that book!'

I shuffled over. The guide – her name was Emmeline – was showing Matthews a bunch of writing.

'Are you interested in *The Book of Thoth?*' she asked me.

I grunted.

'It's explained here – the book that holds all stories was found in the heart of a tree sent from Lebanon – do you see? That's the sign for a tree, that's for book. It's not clear if Thoth wrote it or claimed it . . .'

'So where is it now?' I asked.

'Ah, well – it burned with the great library of Alexandria,' she said. 'Or possibly it was shipwrecked in the Nile. Pity, isn't it? I always wanted to know if it had every story ever told, or every version – if it would have had Shakespeare? And if it had *Romeo and Juliet*, would it have had *West Side Story* as well? And did it give the same story to different people? And how did it decide what story it was going to give who? And if you liked a story, would you ever get it again? There are accounts of it from ancient times, but they don't answer the questions I have . . . Of course, there's also a theory that it survived . . .'

She realized I was looking at her as if she was a total blabbering idiot and she dried up. Honestly – a magic book! Grow up!

Matthews though was continuing. 'Probably they were all in ancient Egyptian hieroglyphs though, so most of us would need a translator anyway . . .'

'But if it was from Lebanon it would not have been in Egyptian. I read a theory once that it was actually from Mesopotamia . . . that it might have been the origin of the opening of the Gospel of St John, you know – "In the beginning was the Word, and the Word was with God, and the Word was God". Maybe it has different languages . . . And sometimes it's a clay tablet; sometimes a papyrus – oh, there's loads of stories . . .'

I tuned out. Stories were all very well, but the Bible! How dull can you get!

That night, I woke from a deep dream with a start and a yelp. A green-eyed woman had been speaking to me, holding out a book on a tasselled pillow and saying, 'You can have everything.' A bird-headed god had come and chased her away.

I was sweating and breathing hard.

A book with every story in it! New stories every time!

Dad would like that, I thought. I bet there'd be a story in there good enough to publish. I could get that book and give it to Dad.

I told him about it when we got back to Cairo.

'That sounds great, Jellyfish,' he said. That's what he called me when – when we played together. We did, sometimes. 'It sounds a very useful book. You find it and bring it to me, eh?' And he tickled me.

For the rest of my life, the idea of the book didn't leave me alone.

CHAPTER 9

Lee

Tired!

Corpus Christi Mariani! I wasn't tired!

I was in criking shock.

I'd spent the day chatting with a book!

Listen – a lot of you, probably, can read. You're likely to be accustomed to reading, or to listening to stories, on CDs or by your parents or whatever. I was not accustomed, in the first place, even to stories. Apart from that month with the *Beano*, Mum never read to us. Dad? Don't make me laugh. The whole story thing, if I knew of it at all, was just Dad and the uncles and Granddad Fred drinking beer and going on about stuff that happened a hundred years ago down the shores. So for a start to have that story about strangling the lion, and then all that life story of the book – told me by the book!!!! And then me piping up with all these questions and the book just breaking off his story to answer me . . . Well, I imagine you can understand I was amazed. On several levels.

And then he decides I'm tired and shuts down. Well,

that's not right. If there's one thing I know, it's that if you can read you can read anywhere, any time, for as long as you want till the story's finished, and even then you can go back to the beginning if you so choose. So I didn't think much of that.

But oh, my days.

I used him as my pillow again. He hadn't objected. Also I wanted him close. It was an instinct.

It wasn't till the next morning that things started to fall into place. The night before, I had finally gone to sleep full of glitter and wonder at the fabulous thing that was happening to me. In the dawn, as I lay achy and half awake, watching the light begin to appear like ghostly smoke down the ventilation shaft, practical thoughts came to me.

One, my new friend had a price on his head of 25,000 dirhams. OK, I'd been tempted. I'm a thief! I steal things – that's what I do. But now . . .

Well, you don't sell your friend, do you? If someone doesn't talk to anybody for 12,000 years, and then they talk to *you*, do you sell 'em? No, you don't. It ain't right.

I never, ever, ever was going to give him up. Unless, I don't know, destiny or something needed him. Or if Nebo turned up on Mushusshu, saying, 'Oi! That's my sacred tablet.' Then I might. Probably I'd have to.

Otherwise, no. It felt more than a bit peculiar turning down more caio than I've ever dreamed of. But there you go.

Two, Jenny Maple. The description had rung a bell yesterday but I hadn't heard it clearly. Now it was blatant: Julie Mordy, Ciaran's mate from Kennington, used names that matched her initials. She was fifteen or so, quite little, and had this knack of looking really innocent, which helped her a lot in her career of small-scale crim activity. Julie's speciality was running errands for people and seeming clean.

So how was she mixed up in this? Why did the police want her?

Something else had struck me. If Mr Ernesto had given the book – I really had to work out what to call him – to this author, whatsername, then why had he not actually given him to her? Why did he still have him on him, and why did he leave him with Mr Maggs? And why did he get killed? And why did he shout 'Elly-Anne'? Who was that?

Also, Ms Author had to be a pretty bad author if she couldn't even think up something more original than 'my heart goes out to his wife and family at this difficult time'.

The book, it occurred to me, would be able to tell me. He was telling me his life story after all – he would have loads of information about Mr Ernesto.

I got up and stretched myself and rinsed my mouth and had some breakfast. Never had the prospect of a day all alone underground been so enticing. I picked up my new friend.

'Good morning, Booko,' I said cheerfully.

'Booko!' he squeaked. 'Absolutely not. You can't call me Booko! You're going to have to come up with something better than that, for crike sake.'

CHAPTER 10

The Story According to Billy Raven

My brother Lee's a good boy, nobody's saying he ain't. Well, I'm not. He's a good boy. He just ain't the brightest. We're a big family, everybody can't be the brightest and in our family it's Lee.

Here's an example: Lee won't go to school. Well, that ain't very bright.

Here's another: he won't stay home. There's Mum loves all her boys, worried sick about him; and there's Dad, who'll give him no end of grief when he gets hold of him, which he was always going to and you can bet your aunt Fanny he's going to now . . . that ain't very bright.

And here's another. Lee'll always use the same fake name. Hello, Lee! If you use Joe English all the time, guess what, we know it's you!

Lucky Dad's in Paris, that's all I can say. Lucky Squidge and Finn and Ciaran listen to sense and are letting me handle this. Lucky Mum's in the way of being – how can I put it? – obedient to whoever she thinks is the alpha male in the area. I.e., for the moment, Dad being away, me.

So when young Joe English is all over the papers in charge of a valuable manuscript and wanted by the old bill, it is my honourable duty to go and bring him in.

The rules are simple when you're looking for someone. Where was they last seen? So I took myself to Berkeley Square, to the booksellers.

It was evening by the time I got there. A young lady responded. She wouldn't open up; only talked through the intercom.

'Yes?' she says, all high and mighty.

'I'm here about the manuscript,' I said, in my best posh English – learned, I may say, at school off the chaplain, realizing as I did that talking proper is a skill like any other and worth having in your repertoire.

'What about it?' she said. *Her* posh voice sounded completely natural. To the manner born.

'I believe I may have some information which may be of interest to you,' I said, which was true, but I wasn't going to give it her – quite the opposite, I was going to get some off her.

'Then you should go to the police,' she said. Lovely! People are so easy to read, ain't they? I love straight people. So simple.

'I'm afraid that's not possible,' I said regretfully. 'For reasons into which I cannot go in public, I am unable to talk to the police. If, however, you would let me in for a moment I could explain to you.'

I waited a moment or two while she no doubt looked me up and down on her little screen inside and made her decision. My guess was that, like all respectable people involved in a mystery, she wanted to solve it. Villains and people with secrets don't do that. They just move on, quickly, with no comment except perhaps a quick 'none of my bliddy business, mate'.

My guess was right. She buzzed open the door and stood inside to greet me.

She was gorgeous, I have to say. Younger-looking than she sounded, Indian, with long smooth black hair and big suspicious eyes. For a second I was about to flirt with her but I pulled myself together just in time. Time and place, Billy Boy. Not here and not now, that's for sure.

'Well?' she said rudely.

'I know Joe English,' I said. 'If you can tell me exactly what happened, I can work out where he might have gone.'

'And you are?' She wasn't giving an inch.

I smiled ingratiatingly.

'I'm his social worker,' I said, in a concerned and kind way. 'Richard Oliver's the name. Joe has had a lot of problems and he needs help. I very much want to get to him before the police, for his own protection. He's not a bad boy . . .' I find this approach often works with females, who like to think the best of everybody, and exercise their sympathy and redemption and that stuff. With guys I'd say I *was* the police and wanted to put the little graspole away before all them lefty liberal social workers let him off his crimes and sent him on holiday to Tenerife on account of his hard childhood . . .

I had misjudged.

'Not a bad boy?' she said. 'He's a little thief and possibly a murderer.'

'Well, yeah, of course, there's that,' I said, stumbling a bit over how to change tack. 'So it's vital he's got off the streets . . .'

'Of course it is,' she said. 'I don't need you to come round here to tell me that.'

She had this disconcerting way of just saying things blankly, like that. No 'yeah well maybe' or 'I think' or 'it could be' or 'do you agree?' Just straight out, unadorned.

Either that or her beautiful black eyes was getting to me. I was not coming over as the suave and effective Billy Raven I usually am.

'So could you tell me what happened?' I said brightly. Or weakly.

'I thought you had information for me,' she said.

'I just told you,' I replied. 'Hard life, deprived kid, all that.'

'That is of less than no interest to me,' she said. 'I just want the book back. If you can tell me where he might be, then I'm interested.'

'Well, perhaps I can,' I said. 'If you can tell me where he went when he left this house.'

She had a think. It suited her. Then: 'Well, it's in the public domain,' she said. 'He went down to Piccadilly, turned left, got into conversation with a boy and they disappeared up a side street opposite Lansdowne Row. He hasn't been seen since.'

I smiled. It was as I had thought.

'Madam,' I said, laying it on a bit, 'I may indeed be able to find young Joe and get your book back. Leave it with me.' And I scarpered.

CHAPTER 11

The Story Continues According to Janaki

Well, I wasn't letting him get away with that. There were altogether too many people turning up on our doorstep lying. Social worker indeed!

The boy had obviously stolen the book because that's the kind of boy he was. Those people would steal anything that wasn't nailed down – it's second nature to them.

Then the girl, Jenny Maple – well, she was something else. Mr de Saloman was already dead by the time she came round with her fake letter, asking for the book! Who was she? Why did she want the book? Where did she get that letter? You may think it was none of my business but personally I felt some responsibility. Mr de Saloman had left his book with the House of Maggs, so we are meant to protect it. Mr Maggs looks to me for organization and good advice, and I am honour-bound to Mr Maggs. He is my father now and the House of Maggs is my family.

So I wasn't letting this one get away so easily. Social worker! He had scamp written all over him. Before he'd even turned down Berkeley Square I had my big scarf wrapped round my head, my sunglasses jammed on the front and I was off after him, just an invisible Asian school-girl going about her business in a bit of a hurry.

I followed him across the square. He turned left up Bruton Lane and by the time I barrelled round the corner he was standing on the pavement, staring at the tarmac in the middle of the road. I backed into a doorway to see what he'd do next.

It was very odd. There was no one around, but he glanced this way and that, then *lay down* in the middle of the road, with his ear to the ground. He seemed to be listening, though what he hoped to hear I had no idea. Then an electro turned into the street and he jumped up again and, looking thoughtful, turned and stared to the north-west. He gave a little snigger of laughter and then he began to walk in the direction in which he had been looking.

I realized that where he had been listening there was a manhole.

I followed him. I wished I'd had a chance to tell Mr Maggs I was going out, but I didn't dare try and ring him. Trying to stay invisible while scurrying along was already hard enough work.

The young man went on up Bruton Lane, through the warren of mewses at Bourdon Street, Avery Row and Lancashire Court, heading in a loop north towards Oxford Street. It was a warm evening and there were plenty of people around. I didn't feel there was any danger, as such, but my heart was pounding.

Crossing Oxford Street, I nearly lost him in the hurly-burly of buses and electrocabs. Heat was rising gently off the pavement and my feet ached a little. I was only really used to being inside at Maggs Brothers. A woman with lots of shopping bags pushed past me and I stumbled – when I looked up, he was nowhere to be seen.

I hurtled to the north side and looked around.

There!

He was going into a cafe. I could see him through the plate-glass window, ordering some food, sitting down. He looked as if he were settling in.

I positioned myself across the road, keeping an eye on him through the rumbling traffic. Now would be a good time to ring Mr Maggs.

He answered almost immediately. 'Janaki, my dear!' he cried. He only ever calls me 'my dear' when he's worried. 'Where are you? The police have been here again and I couldn't find you!'

'Mr Maggs,' I said, 'listen – somebody else came round about the book! He said he's called Richard Oliver and claimed to be Joe English's social worker, but I don't think he is. He said he knew where Joe would have gone, so I've followed him.'

Of course dear Mr Maggs was horrified.

'Janaki!' he cried. 'For goodness' sake, child, come

home! It could be dangerous! Where are you? There is a lot of money at stake here . . . Come home and I will send the police . . .'

'No,' I said, and actually I surprised myself. 'If he's to lead us to the book we don't want him scared off.'

'Oh, for goodness' sake, child,' he said, but then the reception went fuzzy. I was saying, 'I'll call you later' – and we were cut off.

Could I really follow him myself, alone? Wasn't I too scared? I didn't know.

Somehow I stayed where I was.

Every now and again Richard Oliver looked up and out at the street. He lingered over his meal. Then, when it was pretty much dark, he paid and came out of the door.

It occurred to me that he had been waiting for the dark.

So I was going to follow him at night-time.

OK. I could handle that. It would make it easier to hide from him.

He was turning into a small street. Slowing down.

I followed. It was a cul-de-sac, widening out at the end into a kind of small square, with one imposing building taking up the end. Along the sides were Georgian buildings like Maggs Brothers: brown brick, handsome, with black iron railings in front and steps down to the area below. Several of them had blue plaques to show what famous people had lived there in the past. The windows of the office buildings all had a shut-up Sunday look: blank-faced. There were fewer people here. One of them was Richard Oliver.

The moment there were none (except for me, pressed invisibly against a doorway again), he crossed over to the last house on the left and neatly jumped over its railings.

What was he up to?

I crept along to the building and, positioning myself silently on its pale stone steps, I peered over into the dimness of the area.

He was down there and beside him was a manhole. He swivelled his head up in a last-minute check and then, swift as a monkey, he had twisted off the manhole cover and jumped down.

All that was left was a hole in the ground.

I couldn't quite believe what I had just seen. It seemed impossible, somehow. People don't just disappear down holes. I stared at the empty space where he had been. After a few minutes it became clear that he wasn't imme-diately just going to pop out, so, cautiously, I approached and crept down the iron stairs.

The manhole cover lay on the ground where he had left it: dull grey metal, with Dudley and Dowell written on it.

I stepped carefully over it and peered down the hole.

How could Mr de Saloman's book possibly be down there?

CHAPTER 12

The Story Continues According to the Book

Booko! Well. Honestly. Made me sound like a footballer.

He was going to have to come up with something better than that.

Actually – I was rather excited about the idea of having a name. While I was closed I had been thinking of what might be good ones. Something in Babylonian, perhaps, to convey my roots. But nobody would be able to pronounce it. But then – well, realistically, nobody would need to apart from the boy. I wasn't suddenly going to become a public chatterer, natter natter natter with everyone I came across. No, this boy would be the only one to ask me questions. This was not my choice. It was how things were. I am after all a book. I communicate on the page – even when I really love my reader, and there have been some I have loved very much, the ones who discovered my secret and returned to me over and over.

But . . . many children can't read. Adults too.

If I come across them in the future, might I not speak to them, now that I have found my voice?

The idea scared me a little. Not because of talking to them, but because . . . well. Put it this way. It is not a nice feeling to be coveted by men. When they covet you they steal you and chase you and do all sorts of alarming things, and you cannot always protect yourself. If you try to, you can draw even more attention. You have to find someone to protect you. Would this boy be able to protect me? It was a long time since I had been through a metamorphosis – I had held the same basic shape now since I became vellum sixteen hundred years ago. The occasional temporary swap into modern book form – that funny *Beano*, for example – was nothing much to me. But what if they wanted to make me digital, technological? I had evolved from clay to papyrus to vellum long ago, in my youth . . . Could I now become bytes or bits? A disc or a pod, like the boy said – a pod full of binary code? This has been beginning to happen to stories. They are taking another new form . . . I had changed before and I will change again no doubt. Even so, I shivered a little at the thought.

Am I ready to become a piece of technology?

I think not. I think humans still love to read words from paper pages.

I had been lonely beyond belief locked up for years by those de Salomans, with no one to offer a story to – except when my darling Eliane came to me of course, breaking the rules and not being scared of her great-grandmother's curse. I gave her a pink fluffy cover once – oh, she was so happy. But all those stories about ballerinas I had to think up! And now I was out in the world again . . . Well, it was exciting. But alarming. I was made for the study, the deckchair, the bedside table – not for the sewer and the ambitions of modern science.

Still, here was my nice new reader. My new friend, I could call him even. I was in his hands and I would give him what he wanted. He wanted to know the very most recent part of my tale. He wanted the bit with him in. Humans always do. Usually I manage to give it to them – or at least, to paraphrase the philosopher Jagger, if I don't give them what they want, I give them what they need. But what I can't do is cut to the end. Read me and you read in the right order. No cheating.

So I told him first about life in the tomb in Egypt, and about the earthquake that came and ripped our quiet life-in-death to shreds, and how I lay in my pot for years under the desert sands. I told him about being dug up by that thieving skinny-legged graverobber, and how he ran into the governor's agent at a tavern and the governor's agent scared him into handing me over, and how the governor's agent sent me to Zenodotus, the librarian at Alexandria, in case I was valuable. At Alexandria I was loved. The Pharaoh, Ptolemy I, was a demi-god with a beaky nose; he loved books so much that every ship which came to Alexandria was searched for books, and every book that was found he bought it, or stole it, or had it copied. This is how his library became one of the wonders of the world.

'So you've known lots of gods?' he said.

'Of course,' I replied.

'Weird,' he murmured. 'Go on.'

'Zenodotus soon discovered my nature,' I continued, 'and gave me directly to Ptolemy, who kept me for his personal pleasure, reading my stories every night, and telling nobody of my magic properties – not even Demetrius of Phalerum, whose idea the library had been in the first place. He only told his son, Ptolemy II. He's the one who bought Aristotle's library.'

'Who's Aristotle?' he asked.

'That's another story,' I said.

'Only my brother Billy uses it for rhyming slang – Aristotle, bottle, bottle and glass, ar–'

'Yes, well, thank you for that,' I said. 'Moving swiftly on . . . Ptolemy II loved me too, but he had to hide me from Ptolemy III, who had passionate but – curious – literary habits. He stole some very valuable stuff from the Athenian State Archive – originals by Aeschylus, Euripides and Sophocles . . . Do you use those for vulgar terms as well?'

I was actually rather interested. Slang was one kind of use of language that I tended to miss out on.

'Well, there's a knock-knock about Euripides . . . You know knock-knock jokes?'

'Of course,' I replied with dignity.

'OK. Knock, knock.'

'Who's there?'

'Euripides.'

'Euripides who?'

'Euripides pants one more time Eumenides pants yourself!'

Well, I laughed and laughed. Having known them, you know – it sent me quite back to old times. Lee, I have to say, didn't think the joke was funny at all. But he liked the fact that I did. I was shaking with laughter and he was delighted with that.

'You're moving!' he cried.

'Yes,' I said.

'That is brilliant,' he said. 'What if I tickled you? Would you feel it?'

'I –' I managed to say, but he was already having a go, tickling up my spine with his little fingers . . .

'Get off!' I yelled, with no dignity whatsoever. 'Stop that! Stoppit!'

'Oh, my days, you're ticklish!' he squeaked, as I wriggled and giggled and winced. 'And you're moving! Ha ha ha ha! There's a book having hysterics on my lap!'

'It's not fair!' I squealed. 'I ca-a-an't – I can't get you back! Stoppit!!!!'

In the end he did.

I was panting and hiccuping, and he was grinning.

'That's very funny,' he said, with his huge smile.

'Well, I'm glad you think so,' I said, as I got my breath back.

'Well, it is,' he said. 'Anyway, when did you last have a good laugh?'

It was a fair point. I had not laughed for several centuries.

After a while I took up the story again.

'It was beautiful in the Ptolemies' royal enclave,' I said. 'We lived in marble halls, with courtyards and fountains, rugs and statues, peacocks and rare beasts. There were 500,000 scrolls and codices and papyrus scrolls. But it wasn't a safe place. Zoilus had his head chopped off for joking about Ptolemy II marrying his sister. Ptolemy II poisoned Demetrius too. They said he was bitten by a snake while he was having his siesta, but he was poisoned.

'The Ptolemies went downhill from there. Numbers IV and V were weak and useless. Number VIII married a sister who'd been married to their other brother before and then married his niece. The last of them was Cleopatra – ah, there's a story.'

'I know about her. She got rolled up in a carpet with no clothes on as a present for the Roman emperor. Then she got bit by a snake.'

'Well – yes. There is a little more to it than that.'

'Will you tell me, later?'

'Of course,' I said.

'So what happened then?'

'Ptolemy II had always been very secretive with me. He hid me away and as a result, after he died, nobody knew about me. I had been forgotten in a box. Luckily, in fact for me, because the box was kept in the Sister Library, up the hill at the Serapeum, so when Julius Caesar came and set fire to the boats in the harbour and the flames licked up and caught the docks, and the warehouses, the Museion and the main library too . . . I was safe, but everything else burned. By mistake, they said. Thousands and thousands of books. Seven hundred thousand. The wisdom of the past rising in columns of black smoke on the wind . . .' It hurt me still to think of that fire. The smell of it, the crackle and thump and howl.

The boy put his hand softly on my page.

'Well, I survived. Then in AD 385 I was stolen by some lunatics inspired by mad Bishop Theophilus. More book-burners. These ones were burning everything except the Bible. Only the Bible could be true, they said. All other wisdom was pagan, and therefore wrong, and had to be destroyed. *Eheu* . . . dark days. Alexandria sank back to nothingness. Mud and silt blocked the Canopic Nile, the Hepastadium was covered over, and the sea crept in. Sphinxes lay abandoned on the seabed. The fanatical Emperor

Theodosius, the beautiful philosopher Hypatia, murdered by Bishop Cyril. Later, when the Arabs came, they burned the remaining books to heat the water for their baths.

'I wasn't there for that. A pair of stupid rioters had taken me home as kindling for their domestic fire. They put me on a woodpile outside their hut. The smoke from the burning library and the Serapeum was drifting across the sky. People were coughing from it. I was scared then. I thought I was going to die . . .

'Then, at sunset, an ox came by and ate me.'

The boy laughed. I must say that though he was fascinated by my tale he wasn't entirely respectful.

'It was no laughing matter,' I said. 'Have you ever been eaten by an ox?'

'Course not,' he said. 'But I'm not an ancient magic book.'

'It's still no fun,' I said. 'All that chomping and spit. But being eaten did not, as you will have noticed, destroy me.

'Go on then,' he said.

'The ox that ate me was very fertile and of her calves several were sent to Rome to the vellum factories. And so I became a book again: stretched on wood, smooth and pearly, polished and pure. I bound a notebook for an astrologer. I passed on to a monk who made me the book of his heart and wrote in me each day his sins and his acts of virtue. He believed that God wiped me clean each night, to inspire him to greater virtues. He did become a very virtuous man.

'For many years after his death I stayed in his monastery. Various monks for many years wrote their dreams and sins and aspirations in me. Some of them were poets. Whatever was written, my pages were always clean.

'In the year 1025 I returned to the East, in the pocket of a crusader. I stopped an arrow on the outskirts of Jerusalem, but my owner died anyway. I was taken for a while by a mathematician, till he drowned in a shipwreck and I washed up on the shore of the Black Sea. A bandit took me to Athens and sold me to a woman who wrote songs in me. I was stolen from her purse and brought to a philosopher who wrote in me all his doubts about the purpose of life. He gave me to his son, who sold me to a Frenchman who gave me to his true love – another man's wife – full of the love poems he had written to her while he was at war. Her husband found me and threw me in the midden, where a child spotted me and cleaned me and hid me in her girdle. Her name was Eliane de la Roche. Each day she would take me out and read me and it was she to whom I began to retell all the stories I had learned from humans through the years. It was she whose desire for stories I heard and fulfilled. She was the first since Ptolemy I for whom, each time I was opened, I had a new story.

'She, sweet child, told her father. He beat her and locked me up as a piece of witchcraft.

'The local priest heard of it and confiscated me. I was to be burned – again! – but the darling girl rescued me and gave me to her cousin for safekeeping. He took me to the coast and copied out the stories I produced each day, and gave them to his friends. When he died, I lay in a cupboard for many years. An undertaker found me and when he opened me there were stories on my pages. By now I had no choice: my stories had been woken and all I could do was be read.

'The undertaker sent me to the Pope in Rome. The Pope's Undersecretary for Unwanted Gifts put me in a chamber with all the other unwanted gifts and sent a letter of thanks. The undertaker died mad from never knowing what the Pope thought of me. Some years later, a young soldier of the Swiss Guard, sentry to the Chamber of Unwanted Gifts, found me, wrapped in cobwebs, and stole me for his sweetheart. He died, mad from guilt at having stolen from the Pope. His sweetheart died of grief at his death, and her sister tried to tear out my pages, but my story of Orpheus and Eurydice so enchanted her that she could not. Instead she read me every day and was known as an eccentric. Her daughter married a Russian and took me to St Petersburg; her son hid me inside a grand piano and shipped me to Japan.

'Do you want to know it all? All the tears and the fortunes made and lost?

'I was a book which could not die and which had in it

whatever you want. You want to know to whom I belong? And why this latest owner died?

'All I can tell you is that someone is trying to steal me again. Where people used to want to burn me, now they want to sell me for money, or own me for profit. If they don't succeed now someone else will later. But I cannot tell you who they are or what they are doing to try to get me . . .'

'I don't want them to get you,' said Lee. 'I'll look after you.'

The girl had said that too. When they said that it made me want to give them the best stories.

'Thank you,' I said. 'That's kind. You might not be able to, you know . . .'

'Well, you can't look after yourself, can you?'

At that, there was a scrabbling noise from the corner.

'What's that?' he squawked. 'Those bliddy rats again?'

'It's nothing,' I said.

'Only one ran over you while I was asleep,' he said. 'I don't want some rodent nibbling on you . . .' He was looking at me with a very kind expression on his face. 'Listen,' he said. 'You are the most extraordinary thing that has ever happened. You are stupendous. I am just some London kid who can't even read you, and I nicked you by mistake, but now I – Lee bliddy Raven – am responsible for you. You'd've been safe at Mr Maggs, wouldn't you?'

'I believe so,' I replied softly.

'Well, I have to look after you then, don't I? It's an honour.'

'Thank you,' I said. 'Thank you.'

'So carry on then. Where did Mr de Saloman get you?'

'His great-grandfather bought me in an auction in California. I'd been sold in a box by a Japanese woman who'd had to leave after the Second World War. Mr de Saloman's great-grandfather knew she was a relative of the ancestor who had gone to Japan from Russia, so he acquired her things . . .'

'So, did Mr de Saloman give you to Nigella Lurch?'

'He did not,' I said. 'He would never give me to anyone. He protected me. As best he could.'

'Nigella Lurch said in the paper that Mr de Saloman gave you to her as a gift. She's a writer,' he said. 'Is that why she'd want you? Does she know what you really are? How could she? Did Mr de Saloman know?'

'Mr de Saloman did not know,' I said. 'Like most of his family, he was afraid to know. But there are people who know – people who know and don't believe, people who both know and believe. They are the dangerous ones. If people know what I am, and believe it, they want me. If she has heard of me, and traced me, she wants me. To read my stories, or to use my powers, or to sell me.'

I felt a little shiver run through my pages as I said it.

'I want you,' said Lee, and he sounded apologetic.

I said nothing, but I was touched. He wanted me for the right reasons.

Then he asked me, 'Do you know why Mr de Salomar died?'

'Yes,' I said.

'Why?'

'Why do I know? Because it is part of the story and I know all the stories. Why did he die? I cannot tell you. You must find out. That is your story.'

'Won't you tell me my story?'

'It hasn't happened yet,' I told him. 'I can't tell you the story before the story exists.'

He leaned back and thought about that. He was happy.

'Tell me a story,' he said, after a while.

So I did. I told him stories of heroes: James Bond, Achilles, Artemis Fowl, Alex Rider, Tom Sawyer. He soaked them up like a thirsty thirsty child, and at the end of the day he circled me in his arms again and he slept.

CHAPTER 13

Continuing the Story According to Nigella Lurch

One afternoon when I was fifteen my mother sat me down on a little sofa and said to me, 'Nigella, your father is no longer with us.' I was looking at a small teapot on the shelf, with flowers on it, pink and green. I thought she meant he had divorced her and gone away to write properly, without me creeping round his door and spoiling his concentration.

A year later she married some old colonel and moved to South Africa. Left me all alone in London. I was seventeen. About a year after that I realized that really he must be dead.

He hadn't published anything.

I'd done some modelling. Some publicity work. Nobody ever paid me properly though – all the other girls had rich families and they seemed to think I had too.

One man, Hughie, had a grandmother who'd died. She'd left him a chest of old rubbish which he felt obliged to go through, so I helped him just in case there were any emerald earrings in there. It was just old papers. Among them was a file full of stories. I sat there leafing through them while Hughie dutifully looked through all the things he had to look through, waiting for him to finish so we could go out to lunch.

They weren't bad, in quite a childish way.

One of the publicity jobs I'd been sacked from was at a publishing house. I began to have an idea.

I stole the stories and I typed them up – tapping away, just like my father used to. Then I sent them to the publishers I used to work for.

Well, Hughie was livid, but because I had typed them all out and burned the originals he couldn't prove anything.

'She used to tell me those stories about Cotton MacGill the Detective Cat when was I was a kid!' he shouted. 'When I'd go to stay with her, she'd sit on the end of the bed and make them up for me!' But Hughie was an only child, and the old girl was dead, so that was that.

I was delighted by how easy it was for me to be published. Cotton MacGill was tremendously popular. I even promised the publishers more . . . silly of me really. But they were so keen and everyone was so nice to me. There was only one problem really about me being a famous successful writer – I couldn't write. I'd never even tried.

All the respect I had had for writing rather seeped away at that point. I came to think of my father as a poor fool, to have made himself – and my mother – and me! – so miserable over something so cheap.

Once I had a bit of money, I knew just what to do with it. I invested – in all kinds of things. Abroad, mostly. Shops, stocks and shares, property. Casinos. A few little online businesses. Some things that were not so . . . legal. Weapons. Soldiers for hire. A little people-trafficking. I had a friend in the City who tipped me in advance what shares to buy. I became very rich. I really didn't much care about how I made the money. I just wanted more. It became a game. Anything which other people wouldn't get involved in, I'd go in there and make a killing. There was so much opportunity. I married a few times. I changed my name. I became a different woman.

Then something peculiar happened. I used to get terribly bored, so one day I decided to go to see this woman – well, a friend of mine had said she was simply wonderful, quite unbelievable. She was a medium. I trotted into her rather vulgar fringed-curtain-and-chenille-type boudoir, assuming I was wasting my time but rather excited as well. She sat me down at her small table, took my hand and said, 'Mrs Ardleish is extremely angry with you.'

'Oh, nonsense,' I said. 'I don't know any Mrs Ardleish.'

'You stole her cat,' the medium said. She looked up at me and her eyes were bright green. This made me feel very odd.

'I never stole any cat,' I said, and my words faltered, and the green eyes drilled through me, and I remembered my dream in Egypt long ago.

Her eyes dropped to the table. The chenille cloth felt squeaky under my bare elbow.

'Your father doesn't want to talk to you,' she continued. 'He says he can't be bothered.'

'Still!' I shrieked. 'Still! What do I have to do to please him? What more do I have to do!' I was upset by this. My father still too busy to love me.

She took no notice. She carried on talking, murmuring in her peculiar way.

'The thing you doubt exists,' she whispered. 'You can have everything.'

The phrase struck me like a blow to the belly.

Why would she say that, just after talking about my father?

She looked back at me.

'What?' I asked.

'It's not nonsense, the thing you have always wanted. You can have it. You can have everything.'

I knew exactly what she was talking about.

'How do I find it?' I said, and I heard my voice coming out hoarse with excitement.

'How would I know? That'll be fifty dirhams.'

So that was it, for me. My fixation on the book grew. All this money was all very well but I wanted more. Now I had something to spend my money on. I went back to Egypt, to Alexandria, to Paris, to Rome and Washington, I searched every library and every archive and I learned more about this legendary book than anybody had ever known. I frequented auctioneers' showrooms and dusty antiquarian bookshops. I pored and I pored and I pored over catalogues and histories. I let it be known, in select circles, that I was in the market. I was brought nonsense at silly prices, and I turned it away.

If I found what I was looking for, I could be a writer again. If I could be a writer, I could . . .

I didn't find it.

But I was going to.

CHAPTER 14

The Story Continues to Continue According to Lee

My heart was full of the book when I fell asleep – full of the long long time he had existed. I was dreaming of peacocks in marble courtyards, the cries of rioters in the purple night, flames licking in the distance, coming closer, ships burning at sea, salt and smoke smell drifting across the sea, and the threat of blood and the clash of swords . . .

I was deep in my dreams.

I tossed and fretted, and I didn't sleep long.

Something woke me. Someone – landing on me, squealing, and then swiftly scrabbling away. It was dark. I flailed about, reaching – something was missing.

The book.

Not in my arms.

Not within reach.

I found the torch and flicked it on. The book was gone.

I howled and jumped up.

The manhole lid was still clanging. I grabbed for my skello – gone too. But someone was still there.

'Where's my book?' I yelled. 'Give it me.'

It was a girl. She was cowering in a corner, her knees pulled up, her eyes glowing like an animal. 'I don't have it,' she gasped. 'He's got it.'

'Who?' I was still half asleep, but that didn't stop me from racing up the ladder and banging and banging at the manhole cover till my fists hurt.

'How on earth would I know?' she said.

I climbed down again. Whoever had done it wasn't going to come back out of kindness and mercy, were they? And if somebody else heard, what good would that do? Less than none. I'd be saved, yeah, and handed over to the police?

I turned the torch on her. She was staring at me. 'You're in such trouble,' she said. 'I know who you are. I know what you did. He's going to get the police now and —'

She was about my age, wrapped in a scarf, Asian-looking, nicely spoken.

Who the crike was she?

'Police?' I said.

'Of course,' she replied.

'Yeah, great,' I said. 'Thanks. You put the kettle on for them then, eh?' I grabbed my stuff, pulling on my waders and my mask, and slid the lid off the route back into the Tyburn. The smell nearly knocked me backwards. I aimed my torch and I skedaddled.

It's one thing going down the shores at leisure. Bad

enough, you'd think. Going down with some damn foo
unprotected girl following you is another.

Yeah, she came after me.

What could I do? I yelled at her to go back. I could
hear her, retching and stumbling, and I raced ahead so
she'd be scared and turn back of her own accord. She
could bang at the manhole cover, couldn't she, until
someone came? Why the crike was she following me?

My head was in a muddle. One: deal with being below
Two: who was it who'd nicked the book? Three: what the
heck was I going to do now?

I followed the way I had come, easier now going downhill, till I came to the Air Street turn-off. No point coming
out back at Piccadilly. And how was I going to get out
anyway without my skello?

I leaned back against the filthy wall, and shone the torch
down at my feet.

Air Street is narrower than the Tyburn. I had to hold my
neck at a weird angle to make any kind of speed at all. It's
hard to judge distance in the dark, underground, but by
pace-counting I reckoned I was approaching Piccadilly Circus.
Yeah. Think, Lee. Use that useful memory of yours.

The girl caught up with me. She stood close, just outside
the circle of torchlight. She was almost in tears, coughing
and swallowing.

'Spit,' I said. 'Spit the taste out of your mouth, pull yer
scarf across and breathe through yer mouth.'

Her eyes caught a gleam of my torch, black in the blackness, and she did as I told her.

'You going back?'

She shook her head.

'For crike sake,' I muttered.

I started off walking again, neck cricked, waders
sloshing, face wrapped. Within minutes my torch's beam
reflected on the deeper channel and higher roof of the
Shaftesbury Main. I hesitated a moment at the junction,
where the Newport tunnel and the Air Street curved in
to join the bigger one, their trickles of sludge speeding
up a little on the bend and being taken up by the thicker,
darker, deeper, more revolting sweep of the flow in the
Shaftesbury.

I knew where I was heading. I was going up the Shaftesbury
to Frith's Illicit, the cleanest sewer in London. There's a legend
about Frith's Illicit, about gangsters and nightclubs and secret
access. It was illegally built in the 1680s, and it never got
incorporated into the main system, and it's not been used
since hundreds of years ago. Or so my granddad used to say.
I'd never been there. But Granddad Fred knew what Frederick
Bryden knew and now I just had to put my faith in them.
And I had faith, all right. It's all still there, under your feet.
Back in the old days, you'd hide your lamp going under a
grid so no one above would see you glittering in the gutter.
Now no one thinks about it. But it's all still there.

The girl was still rattling along behind me. Shite. She's

pretty brave though. Brave as in totally ignorant. Probably she ain't got a clue what the risks are.

I slowed down. I wasn't going to lose her anyway. Plus I needed to keep my wits about me. Can't be far now. If it's true. I stepped across to a place where the water looked shallower and landed with a crunching on something – things – that moved under my feet. A crackly wet wriggling feeling.

Cockroaches. The big Chinese ones, at a guess.

Behind me I heard a yelp. She'd trodden on them too.

Didn't slow her down though.

In fact she was catching up with me. And still yelping. Behind me I could hear her sloshing and panting. She was calling out. 'Joe!' she yelled. 'Joe!' She sounded, to tell the truth, terrified.

Really terrified.

She was hurtling up on me. And behind her there was another noise – a snorting, groaning, grunting noise, a hungry, greedy, animal noise . . .

Suddenly I was wide awake.

I knew that noise. It was mixed with splashing and quick, heavy, rhythmic footsteps, and it was echoing in the filthy curve of the tunnel, but I knew it anyway. I'd heard it on a wildlife programme. It was –

'They're behind us!' she yelled. 'There's loads of them. Get a move on – quick!'

What I'd heard was wild boars. So this was – Mariani, it

was the pigs. The famous legendary feral pigs of the Fleet.

I pushed her ahead of me and cried, 'Run! Next left. Move it!'

No wonder she hadn't noticed the cockroaches.

We ran, shite flying from where our feet fell, the torch beam bouncing ahead of us on the filthy gleaming wall, and the pigs catching up with us behind. The noise was horrific – spooky and greedy at the same time, and the echoey tricks of the tunnel sent it up ahead of us too, so it seemed to be coming from all round us.

'They're up ahead as well!' she shrieked.

'No, they ain't,' I squawked. 'It's a trick of the sound. Just keep on.'

Crike, how fast do they run? Better be true what they said about Frith's Illicit, that's all. Else we're pigfood.

'Left here!' I yelled. Here we go – heading north. The air was still horrible. Should be along here, left again.

I paused for a second, my breath coming in ragged gasps, and shone the torch up. If this was the Illicit, well, it's been connected now, Granddad. It was filthy. I flicked the torch beam up and around. The tunnel widened out a bit. Brickwork wasn't bad, if it was seventeenth century. Four hundred years of shite has a way of wrecking your tiling, but this looked all right.

'Come on,' I cried, and pushed her up the sewer. It got smaller quite quickly. I flashed the torch around as best I could.

Ah.

Yes!

Iron bars in the wall. Steps.

'Up!' I yelled, and went to push her up the ladder – only she'd already scrabbled up it like a squirrel and had her hand reached down to help me up.

I grabbed it and launched myself up.

Just in time.

'They'll follow us!' she shrieked.

They didn't. They flowed under our feet, a river of fearsome, stinky, grey shadows. The torch beam picked out a slavering wet snout here, a dirty hairy rump there, a pair of creased and greasy ears.

Some of them had tusks.

'They can't tell our smell over the shite,' I said. 'They're not the brightest.'

I was breathless and my heart was going like crike. I was still holding on to her hand. I let go.

'My days,' she said, quietly.

We stared after them. It was quite a mob.

She had her cloth up over her face again.

'Will they come back?' she said.

'Don't matter if they do,' I said, and it didn't, because I had just spotted exactly the thing I had been looking for. I just said to her, 'Here, hold this', and shoved the torch at her. 'Shine it up on this grating.'

She was so surprised she did what I said, and I was able

to climb up over her and check out our chances.

Well, there it was. The legendary grating which the legendary gangsters used in the old days for whatever legendary nefarious purposes of their own. It probably had been opened in the last hundred years, but that's not to say it was oiled and ready for me. I got out my knife and began to scrape at the years of filth and rust that was crusted on the hinges and lock.

'Oi!' she yelled. 'That's going on me!'

'Well, shift over then,' I said. 'And keep yer voice down.'

To do her justice, she did as she was told.

I scraped. She breathed. As my eyes got used to the dimness beyond the grating I could start to make out shapes.

It took a long time. I had blisters on my fingers, the cut on my thumb opened up again, and I wasted Finn's last roll by using the mayonnaise as lubrication on the hinges. But I got it open.

I pushed it up and another shower of rust and dust and grease fell over us both. Then I clambered through. Without being invited, the girl climbed up behind me.

'Where are we?' she asked very quietly.

'In a cellar,' I said shortly. The question was, what cellar? 'Be quiet.'

I took the torch off her and shone it slowly around. The room was small and completely dark. The floor was stone, old, dirty. The walls were invisible behind stacks and stacks of boxes – old, old cobwebby, rotting boxes. Where the sides of the boxes were falling away, their faded writing peeling off, I could make out – what?

I rubbed one with my fingertip. Glass. It was stacks of bottles. Wine bottles.

There was a door on the far side. I glanced back at the grating behind us. For a moment the beam of the torch caught the water down below, sending back a flash of glistening reflection.

I shivered. The smell was of damp and mould and long long ago cold.

I thought of the book – of its years in the Egyptian tomb. The thought twisted the dagger in my heart. I'd said I'd look after him. I'd let him down. I was everything my dad ever said I was. Useless, useless, can't do a single blind thing to save yer life, stupid bliddy useless . . .

Don't go there, Lee. Not now. Don't go into those thoughts. You've got work to do.

I crossed to the door and the girl was right behind me.

The handle came off in my hand – not that it mattered, because so did the door, when I pushed it.

What the door led into was the most curious thing I had ever seen in my life.

CHAPTER 15

And According to Janaki

It was really quite extraordinary. I thought I was seeing things to be honest. I thought I'd become hysterical and was having hallucinations. I was just standing there, peering at the manhole down which 'Richard Oliver' had disappeared. Then there was a pale, pale face coming up at me out of the hole, and I was so shocked that for a moment I forgot to run. When I did it was too late: he grabbed me and I twisted but he had me and he shoved me down the hole, my hair and feet all over the place, my head banging, my elbows scraping and my glasses gone flying. Then he was gone, and I landed on something warm and angular and kicking – Joe English! And then he pushed me o and hurtled down a dark corner and for some reason I don't quite understand even now, I followed him.

Oh, I do understand. I followed him because I was so scared of being left where I was – in an underground chamber with the clanging of the closing manhole lid still echoing above me. I thought, in my moment of panic, that he must know what he was doing. If I'd known he was going down into the sewers of London, I would never, never have gone down there. And once I followed him, and smelt that smell, and realized what I had let myself in for, it was too late. I didn't know how to get out. I'd get lost. Even if I got back to the underground room I couldn't get out of there – I'd seen him try. So I followed him. He must be going somewhere.

I realized, pretty quickly, how bad things really were for me. That smell. The feeling beneath your feet. He had these big boots on but I was just in my shoes. Never, never have I experienced anything so unpleasant. And scary. Ahead of me his torch beam lit up the walls for a moment here, a moment there, as he twisted and turned down the tunnel. I caught glimpses of brickwork, wet and cold and curving. ·

He was quick, too. I called out to him to wait but the echoing noise of my own voice just filled me with more horror. What if I fell? What if I landed in this . . .?

I concentrated on following and keeping up. Just keep up. Don't look, don't think. Don't notice the odd crunch in the silty slime underfoot. Don't think of your hair swinging against the slime. Don't think.

And as for the pigs. I don't even want to . . .

Eyurgh.

It was such a relief when they passed by us. I was almost happy, to hold his torch and have dirt and detritus shower down on to my face as he hacked away. I couldn't clamber up after him quick enough. The filthy wine cellar felt like home after a long journey. I scrabbled my shoes in the dust on the floor, anything to dry them off. I was shaking all over, big jerking shakes.

I threw up, as well. Relief, I suppose.

He glanced at me and handed me a bottle of water from his pack. 'Don't use much,' he said. I rinsed my mouth and spat it out back down the grating.

'Thanks,' I muttered, but he was busy pulling the door to pieces.

And then there we were. He held the torch up high to give maximum light, and we both gasped, and though I was almost in tears, I laughed, and he said, 'Corpus Christi Mariani!'

I had seen places like this before – in the old films Mr Maggs liked to watch on a quiet evening. This was where Marlene Dietrich sat on a high stool on the little stage, while men with hats watched her and smoked, and ladies in smooth satin dresses and feathers drank Martinis. There would be a little orchestra, and people dancing in couples, and sooner or later the men would start to shoot each other. It was an old-fashioned nightclub.

Joe English moved the torch like a tiny spotlight. One by one the accoutrements of the club were lit up. There was the little stage. There was the bar, lined in a thousand mirror tiles, flashing back at us. There was the dance floor. There was the chandelier above it, dripping feathers of dust. There was even a piano, white with dust.

I went over to it. The dust was thick on the lid. I lifted it and a cloud flew up. The piano was still white underneath.

'I wouldn't start playing yet,' he said. I sat on the stool instead and pulled off my shoes and socks.

'Mariani,' he said again, looking around. 'This is absolutely – it's true! It's only true, after all!'

'What's true?' I asked.

'Everything my granddad ever told me,' he said, and that was all I could get out of him.

He went behind the bar and set the torch in the corner, where it reflected back off several mirrored walls. This arrangement gave us a gleaming, fractured, spooky light, but least we could now see the whole place. It wasn't huge, but it wasn't tiny either. Around the dance floor were about thirty circular tables, each with eight little chairs, except the ones round the edge, which had padded banquettes built into the wall. I patted one. The dust erupted and in its place was a handprint showing crimson velvet.

At the back of the stage was a drum kit; behind it on the wall in large curly letters I could read the words 'The Mandrake Club'.

In the middle of each round table was a vase of dead flowers, drooping, stiffened. Set around them were slender, elegant glasses. There were metal buckets on stands, empty bottles. There were plates, the remains of long-ago food not only dried up but peeling off, and gone. There were ashtrays and napkins and mouse droppings, and at one table a fur coat lay draped like an animal killed while trying to escape. At my feet a handbag lay spilled: I reached down and saw a lipstick, paper money and an old-fashioned mobile phone.

Behind the cold and the damp there was a very very faint smell of whisky and cigarettes.

The chill was not just physical.

'What do you suppose happened?' I whispered.

His face was turned away from me and for a while he didn't say anything.

'They left in hurry, at a guess.'

'Why? Why did they leave all their things? Why didn't anyone come back?'

'How would I know?' he said quite rudely.

It wasn't as scary as the sewer, but actually it was quite scary enough. I stood and went round to the back of the bar.

'What you doing?' he barked.

'Thought I'd see if I could clean myself up,' I said calmly. I didn't want to upset him. He seemed quite wound up already. I just wanted to – well, wash the smell of sewer off me. Then I'd think about the situation.

He swivelled round and beat me to the little sink.

Nothing came from the tap but a few peculiar noises. But there was a mass of liquor bottles along the shelves and underneath in the cupboards I found row on row of minerals: waters of various kinds among them.

'Could I use some of this?' I asked him. Maybe if he felt respected he would calm down a bit.

He glanced at the supply. 'Use half a bottle, max,' he said.

I retreated to the privacy of a banquette to clean up my feet and legs. When I'd done, I came back and sat across from him at one of the tables. He'd cleared off the detritus and was resting his head on his arms in a position of utter despair.

He lifted it up and for the first time he looked me in the eye.

'So who are you then?' he said.

'I'm Janaki.'

'And what exactly are you doing here?'

I could feel that my face was trembling. I hoped he wouldn't notice.

'He pushed me down when he went out,' I said finally. 'I was at the top. Then I just followed you – I was scared not to.'

He pursed his mouth a bit.

'What were you doing there anyway?'

I didn't really have much to lose. If he'd wanted to hurt

me he could have left me down the sewer, or let the pigs get me.

'I was looking for you,' I said.

'Why?'

'Because you've got the book.'

He stared at me a while.

'So?' he said.

'You stole it from Mr Maggs.'

'And? Mr Maggs your boyfriend then?'

'He's like my dad,' I said.

For a moment I thought he was going to carry on sneering, but for some reason when I said that, he changed course. He stopped and looked like he was thinking about something else.

'So who was it?' he asked me. 'Who jumped you?'

Well, clearly he could see that I was scared.

'Oh, come on,' he said. 'What difference is it going to make now?'

'He said he was your social worker,' I said.

He laughed. 'That's funny,' he said. 'I've got a social worker. A very kind old bird called Edith, who weighs about eighteen stone and would not be exactly nippy in the getting in and out of sewers department. She ain't seen me for about two years. I don't think it was Edith. What d'he look like?'

I stared at him in the curious torch reflection. 'Go in

the light,' I said, and he moved the angle of his face till it was lit up.

There was no mistaking it. The sticky-up pale hair, the wide eyes, bony cheeks, peculiar pallor.

'He looked like you,' I said.

CHAPTER 16

Nigella Lurch Continues Her Version

It was my thirty-ninth birthday. I was in Rome, celebrating. Some celebration! Nothing to show for my thirty-nine years but some stories published years before. No home, no husband, no child. I had a semi-criminal reputation and masses of money, that was all. My mother hadn't even sent me a card. But then how could she? Not only did she not know where I lived, but she could know nothing of my new identity.

I never used to think about children. Boring little things. But now – I don't know. Everything seems a little superficial. All this pressure of work, and the little treats I give myself don't work to cheer me up any more. I bought myself a little castle in Jamaica and I haven't even been there. Yesterday I'd picked up a new fur coat for my birthday. There it was, flung over the back of the chair. Just a load of dead fur. I wanted things that were alive. I wanted new things. Living things. Clean things.

I wanted to be young again. That's all. Young and clean.

Perhaps I want to be a better person.

With a husband. And children. And a vegetable garden.

But people don't marry an empress of crime. And I can't have children. I could buy some I suppose . . . Not while I'm an empress of crime though. It wouldn't be fair on them. If I were a lady writer now, writing stories about Cotton MacGill the cat . . .

The image had become so clear of late. There I am, sitting at a desk, tapping away, with a child or two playing on the lawn beyond the French windows. Sunshine. No bodyguards, no urgent problems to deal with concerning hitmen in Bratislava. Just a beautiful bunch of flowers from my publishers and a note about a prize I have won. How clean and lovely; how innocent.

And with the book, I could do it.

I wanted it so much. I could no longer push it away. I wanted to be everything my father should have been.

In my stark modern hotel in Rome, my telephone began to ring. It was time for my daily round of calls with my managers around the world. Each of them called me every day at the allotted time. A girl has to keep tight control of an empire like mine.

First I spoke to Zakarias in Budapest. An operative had stolen some money from us.

'Break his legs,' I said.

He had also taken a contact list of my employees.

'Kill him,' I said.

Zakarias was a little reluctant. He suggested perhaps it would be enough just to break his legs.

'Do you want your legs broken, Zakarias?' I said. It no longer thrilled me to say things like that.

He agreed that he didn't.

'Call me when it's done,' I said. 'I shall visit in the next few days to view the body.' You have to keep on top of these things, or people take advantage. God, how boring it all was. I longed not to have to do it any more.

Then I talked to Wang in Beijing. Import/export was going very well, he was happy to report. Profits were up and our bill for bribery was up only 1.5 per cent on the last quarter. This was acceptable. When I hung up I told Maxim, my factotum, to send Wang a big string of pearls as a bonus.

Then I received an unexpected call. It was Adrian in Paris. It was not his turn to call. I shouted at him. He said, 'Madame, I think you will want to hear this.'

I heard him out.

He told me about a girl. She had a brother. He was involved with one of our drug dealers. A rich girl, a desperate brother, an unscrupulous drug dealer. There was a shortage of cash. There was an offer of a book in payment. Adrian felt the book might interest me.

It is my firm belief that if you want something enough you will get it. Desire is a like a magnetic force. For years I had been sending out a call to this book. Recently the call had been getting stronger and stronger. Sooner or later, something will respond.

The sister would be meeting us that night at the Ritz in Paris. I flung my fur around my shoulders and called for my helicopter.

CHAPTER 17

Continuing According to Lee

After the book was stolen from me, after all I'd promised it, I was filled with a kind of pure and righteous anger. I had made promises to that book. I was going to keep those promises.

Like me. The raider looked like me.

Well, that narrows it down a bit.

All us Ravens look exactly the same.

'How old?' I asked her.

'Older than you,' she said.

'But a kid?'

'Eighteen maybe?'

The worst fear slid away. At least it wasn't my dad.

So which one of them? Finn?

Finn knew where I was. He knew the story and the background. I'd told him I didn't have the book, but he might not have believed me. He had a skello.

Well, any Raven can get a skello when he wants one.

And anyone could know the story. If they'd seen the

paper, they could put two and two together and know Joe English was me.

But only Finn knew where I was.

Little graspole, I was starting to think . . . but I wasn't convinced.

I just didn't believe it was him.

Why not?

One, Finn is a bit wet. He's not the bravest, and he ain't got the best skills. I would have woken up if he'd stuck his hand under my head.

Plus, he believes me when I tell him things, Finn and I was always on the same side. Ciaran, now, he'd do anything. No sense of loyalty at all. Not inside the family, anyway. If it's family v. outsiders, obviously we'll all stick together. But inside the family, it's me and Finn, then Billy and Squidge – Squidge'd do anything for Billy, then Ciaran rocketing around doing whatever the crike he likes.

Or Squidge?

No. He wouldn't have the enterprise. He'd talk about it, but he wouldn't get round to it.

That leaves Billy.

Billy, the biggest tosher of the lot. He'd do anything for caio. Best skills too. Billy is an extremely accomplished thief. Fine dipper, top-class housebreaker.

Yeah, Billy.

So he's after the reward. And he can't even be bothered to talk to me about it, make me an offer. He wouldn't know that I wouldn't give that book up for love nor money. He should've suggested a split like Finn did.

He is a naughty boy, our Billy. And now he's made it a straight and blatant competition. All right, Billy. You're on.

The girl was still sitting there. There was a bruise coming up on her forehead, no doubt from where Billy had pushed her down the manhole.

But why had he done that?

I asked her.

She was weighing up her answer.

'Just tell me,' I said. 'You're stuck with me, so just tell me.'

'I'll do answer for answer,' she said. 'It's my turn.'

'All right,' I said. She didn't look like she'd be any trouble.

'Why did you steal the book?' she asked.

'What do you know about the book?' I shot back.

'You first,' she said.

I was about to answer, 'Cos I'm a thief,' but something stopped me. Her honest eyes, I should think. Instead I said, 'I didn't mean to.'

'What d'you mean you didn't mean to?' she yelled. 'People don't nick things by mistake! That's absurd . . .'

'My turn,' I said calmly. 'How do you even know about the book? And don't try and tell me you read it in the paper.' I couldn't ask her straight out if she knew what the book was. That would tell her it *was* something, and a girl like her wouldn't shut up till she'd found out what.

'I live at Maggs and I work for Mr Maggs,' she said. 'You stole it from us and we were looking after it for someone else.'

'Mr de Saloman,' I said.

'What do you know about Mr de Saloman?' she asked.

'I read it in the paper,' I grinned, and she smirked at me.

'So, I've come to get the book back,' she said. 'Now what do you mean you didn't mean to steal it?'

'I was looking at it when Mr Maggs came in the room and I just stuck it in my pocket instead of putting it down,' I said.

'You must have big pockets,' she mused.

'Is that your next question?'

'It's not a question at all,' she snapped back. 'No, next question is, where's the book now?'

'Well, that guy nicked him, didn't he?'

'Is that *your* next question?' she asked sarkily. 'Bit of a waste, as we both know the answer. So, who is he then, and what's he doing with it?'

She was clever. I liked her.

Then she said, 'What do you mean "him"?'

'What?' I said.

'You called the book "him". You said "him" not "it".'

'So my grammar is less than perfect,' I said smoothly. 'Sorry about that. Perhaps I ain't had the benefit of a sprauncy education like what you have.'

But she was looking at me now out of very clear eyes.

They told me, clearly, that she didn't know what the book was. To her, it was just a book.

And I wasn't telling her anything. Nothing about Nebo, nothing about magic, and nothing about how, though I stole the book by mistake, I was no way giving him back.

CHAPTER 18

According to Nigella

Adrian and I were in the bar at the Ritz.
'Martini,' I said to the waiter, as we slid in. I was expectant, happy. I had a strong feeling that this could be it.

'So tell me,' I said.

'She is a very unhappy girl,' Adrian began.

'Do I care?' I snapped. 'Tell me about the book.'

He smiled under his little moustache. Adrian is one of my longest-serving employees. I trust him, inasmuch as I trust anyone. Anyway, I pay him a lot.

'It has been in the family for many years – more than a century,' he said. 'Her brother has stolen family books before to settle his debts. You may remember . . .' And in fact I did. I get all kinds of heirlooms from rich young addicts who can't touch their family money but know how to raid their mother's jewel boxes.

'Oh,' I said. 'That boy. So why do we think this book is different from the other stuff he's fobbed us off with?' They'd been good quality, the other books.

Expensive, rare – but not the only book I am interested in.

'His debt is much larger this time. The threats made to him – and to his sister – are more ferocious. They are absolutely desperate. I said to them, bring the best thing you have, and they looked at each other and tears came to their eyes. He said, to her, "But it's cursed." She said, with some bitterness, "So much the better – they deserve it." And I saw from the look she gave me that she believed in the curse. Knowing that you are interested in books with legends and stories attached . . .'

'What is the curse?'

'No one is allowed to open this book. Nobody may read it.'

I smiled and I wondered.

'What is the name of the family?'

'De Saloman,' he said.

We sat for an hour, beneath the drooping palm. I, who never wait for anyone!

At ten minutes late Adrian began to shuffle his shoes. At twelve minutes he made a telephone call. At fifteen he began to swear, softly, in Russian. After half an hour his face was white, his jaw solid tight and he was muttering death threats.

I merely sat there, looking beautiful, drinking Martinis, and getting angrier and angrier. I do not like to be made a fool of.

But I waited. If this was the real book . . .

At nine fifteen, he received a call.

'London!' he yelped. 'But –' Then he said, 'OK, give me the details.' Then more Russian swearing. Then: 'OK, ninety minutes. Yes, the helicopter. Is Rudolph there? And the girl? OK.'

'Adrian,' I said calmly, 'you have raised my hopes.'

'Yes, Madame,' he said.

'I trust you know my attitude to disappointment, Adrian.'

He gulped. 'Yes, Madame,' he said. 'There will be no mistakes. You can rely on me.'

'I do hope so, Adrian,' I murmured. 'I am quite fond of you, you see, and it would be such a shame . . .' I brushed his moustache gently with my finger, and looked him in the eye. 'I am going to London now, Adrian. Would you like a lift? And shall we meet again tomorrow?' My voice was tight with anger.

So you can imagine my howling, furious disappointment when I heard that a Mr de Saloman had been murdered and a book had disappeared.

'Offer a reward!' yelped Adrian, desperate to save his skin. 'Someone must have it! Offer money!'

'How can Romana Asteriosy associate herself with a murder!' I yelled. 'We might as well put out an announcement that we killed him! Don't be ridiculous!'

And then it occurred to me. Romana couldn't offer a reward — but Nigella Lurch could. I could step back into who I used to be. As Nigella, I could offer a reward for a lost book. I could — clever! — claim it was mine. I could start my return to innocence. Nigella would begin to be real again.

'Adrian,' I said. 'Get me a couple of children — babies. Blonde, grey eyes. Healthy ones. A boy and a girl. The younger the better. And a nanny.'

I smiled.

I picked up the phone to ring my publishers from all those years ago. My life was going to change. I was going to be good, and happy, and innocent, with children. I was going to be a writer.

CHAPTER 19

According to Billy

It's a nice feeling to have 25,000 dirhams' worth of exchangeable property in your bag. Easy tosh, by any stretch. Lee and that bird are stuck down the shores, and it'll take them forever to get out – if they can at all, without me going and opening up for them – by which time I'll have cashed in the goods and everything'll be fine. Lee won't mind too much that I did it without him. I'll pay him o . But with his mug all over the papers he really couldn't have pulled it o himself, could he? Nice bit of work though. Excellent to have that reward o ered, as well. Keeps it nice and clean.

So now – Miss Nigella Lurch. Let's look you up. I'd taken the trouble to remove myself from any of the scenes of the crimes and positioned myself in an Internet caff up Regent's Park way. Couple of minutes on the old WWW should give me the old bird's address . . .

Only it didn't. Usually I can get any information in no time at all, but Miss Lurch was a bit undetectable. Googling her brought up loads of references to online bookshops, reviews, articles, foreign editions . . . no address though. Not even any of that 'Nigella Lurch divides her time between Islington and Tuscany' or 'She lives with her husband George and 93 cats in Hampshire.' I hoped she didn't bliddy live in Hampshire. I didn't want to have to go to the criking country.

Well, I wasn't going anywhere at this rate.

Time to start hacking. I got her publishers' site, and had a sniff around, and was able to get in pretty easily. In-house contacts – there we go.

Nothing.

Author details – surely it'll be there.

Nothing.

Was Ms Lurch hiding herself away on purpose?

Her books hadn't been selling that well lately. The last one was out six years ago.

It was children's books she wrote. The Cotton MacGill Mysteries, about a cat detective. Eight of them, out of what was going to be a series of fifteen. Wonder what happened to the rest . . .

Well, I'd just have to read everything till I got a clue. No one can keep their address a secret forever. Not against my skills, anyway.

I got a coffee and sat down to read 873 interviews with Nigella Lurch – none of them less than four years old. Journalists are very nosy. They'll aways say where someone lives.

They didn't.

And I wasn't going to be calling the police information line. Ravens don't talk to the police.

You know those moments when if you was a cartoon character a light bulb would appear over your head? Well, a light bulb appeared over my head.

So first thing in the morning, I rang up the publishers.

'Hello, could I speak to the publicist responsible for Nigella Lurch please?' I said. I put on another of my voices – languid, know-it-all, posh pretending not to be.

'Oh, yeah, hi,' I said. 'This is Pete Walsh, at *The Times* – yeah, sorry, who am I talking to?'

Her name was Venetia.

'Venetia, hi,' I gushed on. 'Listen, really like to run an interview with Nigella, yeah, Nigella Lurch, fascinated by this reward she's offering, you know, lost book, doing a thing on how people can really really *love* books, and the crazy things that makes us do, and yeah, really really big fans of hers from way back, thought it'd fit in really well, only trouble is, really tight deadline, sorry, today or tomorrow?'

Well, I didn't have to ask twice. She was off like a basket of kittens.

Within an hour she'd called back. As it happened Miss Lurch could fit me in that afternoon, and would I be bringing the photographer, what about hair and make-up? I resisted the temptation to wind everybody up, and said no, we'd just be using the publishers' author photo, thanks.

So it was that I proceeded up to Hampstead and found myself on a rather pleasant street where the houses looked like a Victorian giant had gone a bit mad with a set of red bricks and extra turrets.

Her house had all glossy dark leaves outside, and steps up. I ding-donged and an automated voice came on the intercom.

'If you have an appointment, press one. If you represent a public service provider, press two to make an appointment. If you have a delivery, press three. If none of the above, go home and apply in writing.'

I decided to be a delivery and pressed three.

'If you need a signature, press one. If you don't, leave it under the stairs to your right.'

I pressed one. I needed a human being.

For a while, nothing. I rang again.

Then I heard a voice inside.

'Maxim! Maxim, where the heck are you?'

More silence.

Then suddenly the door flung open. It was a woman. A very beautiful woman – not young, but very well presented. Her hair was like Mr Whippy ice cream, blonde, in a pile, waving up and up. You half expected a chocolate flake to be sticking out the side. Her face was a film star's – wide curvy red mouth, smoky eyes turning up at the corners

— but it was all a little smeary, a bit out of focus. Her body was as curvy as her mouth, with added oomph. She was wearing some kind of lady's gown type thing, all silky and not entirely covering her up. It was turquoise, with dragons on it. She was smoking.

'This had better be good,' she drawled.

'Mrs Lurch?' I asked chirpily.

She stared at me. 'I see no package,' she said.

'Well, technically I've come to interview you,' I said. 'But since you mention it, I have got something for you. Question is, have you got what you promised you'd give for it?'

She gave me a deep, dark look.

'Ah,' she said. 'Do come in.'

I followed her into a remarkably fine-looking house. Plenty of nice stuff that I'd have away if that was still my line of work. I took some mental notes to sell on – there's always somebody wants to know the layout of a prosperous house and the potential tosh.

We went into a sitting room with white sofas and a glass table. She pulled a string to roll up the blinds over the windows and afternoon sun flowed in to reveal a scene of glamorous squalor. Empty champagne bottles, glasses with lipstick smudges on the edge, ashtrays full of butt ends also with lipstick on the ends. A big fur coat lay like a puddle on the floor where someone had dropped it. A bottle of perfume seemed to have spilt and the place reeked of its sweet, heavy smell. I stepped back instinctively and she shot me an evil glance.

'Do sit down,' she said, in a rather silky voice.

I sat, or rather perched, on the edge of a huge white sofa. There seemed no question but that if I leaned back it would eat me alive.

'So,' she said, shovelling a pile of magazines to one side. 'Are you the man from the magazine? It's so good to see you. As you know, I have been very quiet for a few years, lying fallow, you know. But now I am ready to start writing again and there will be a new Cotton MacGill story out pretty soon . . .'

I smiled at her. I could see she was playing safe. 'Great,' I said. 'But actually, and sorry to disappoint because of course your literary career is quite fascinating, it's the . . . other matter . . . I'd like to discuss.'

'Oh?' she said.

'The cash,' I said smilingly. 'I just want to confirm that you'll be giving me 25,000 dirhams when I, er, deliver to you.'

Her eyes slid sideways to my bag and flicked back to me.

'Do you have it with you?' she said. Her voice had gone a little husky. My word, she really does want it.

'Yeah,' I said.

'And you're . . . not wanting to hand it to the police? I am of course cooperating with them . . .'

And I knew straight off that she was not and that the police would never be told by her that the book had turned up

'Well,' I said, 'I'm happy to leave all that to you . . . simpler for me . . . as it's you paying, it's you I'll deliver to. Unless you have any objection . . .'

'None whatsoever,' she said. 'In fact' – and here she lit another cigarette from the butt of the one she had finished – 'it might be best not to mention anything to the police at all.'

'Often the best policy,' I remarked.

She flicked her smoky eyes over to me and we smiled at each other. Things are so much clearer and simpler when you know you're both villains.

'So show me,' she said. She was almost breathless and I wondered if I should up the price.

I took out the book, unwrapped it and laid it before me on the table. I hadn't had a chance to have a good look at it before – well, why should I? I was only interested in the money. It looked old and in decent nick and was worth 25,000 dirhams. But I opened it at a random page so she could see it was the real thing and I glanced down. It was some kind of torture scene – someone was being flogged for having stolen something. The words 'Craven thief, it's only what you deserve' leapt out at me.

I turned the book round and offered it to her.

She sighed, and reached an elegant white hand out to the book.

I coughed.

'Cash?' I murmured.

She looked at me, smiled, tightly, and with real physical effort pulled her hand back. Then she stood and went across to a mirrored cabinet, opened a drawer and pulled out several wedges of full-on caio. Returning to the other sofa across from me, she counted it out and then placed it in a pile in the middle of the table. She looked over and gave me a pussycat smile.

She pushed the pile of money towards me.

Despite all our nice manners both of us, at the last minute, grabbed at what we wanted.

She laid her hands firmly over the book. I tucked the caio inside my jacket. Each with our booty in hand, we couldn't wait to put distance between us.

'Bye then,' I said on the doorstep. 'Nice doing business.'

'Bye,' she said, and as I turned to walk away I heard her squawk, 'Jenny? Jenny!' at the top of her voice, back into the house.

CHAPTER 20

Continued by Mr Maggs

By midnight I felt very bad. Janaki was not back. Though I had had quite enough of the police, with Mr de Saloman's dreadful death, and the theft of the book, and discovering that the boy Joe English had left a wallet stolen from the Russian millionairess in my study, I clearly had to call them again.

They told me young girls often disappeared, perhaps she had gone to a nightclub, did she have a boyfriend? I explained that Janaki was not that type of girl but they clearly thought I was an old buffer and a fool, and then wanted to know why she was living in my house when not a member of my family. I have found that my having won her at poker does not go down well with the constabulary so I reverted to the tragic-orphan-adopted-by-loving-great-uncle variation, which is almost true, and quite true enough for the occasion. God forgive me.

Only the next morning did I get a return call from an officer – Sergeant Foley – who had a head on his shoulders and realized the particular connection of Janaki to the murder of Mr de Saloman. I told him about the social worker Richard Oliver and how she had followed him. He promised they would do everything they could and I was mildly comforted.

I was drinking tea when the next shock came. A knock on the door – I was beginning to dread the very sound, so often had it brought bad news of late.

It was another young person – perhaps eighteen or nineteen. Not the youth English, not Janaki, not the mysterious Jenny Maple. It was a small, slender French girl, with pale skin and dark eyes, and dark shadows under her eyes, and a haughty manner. She introduced herself as Eliane de la Roche de Saloman.

I took her upstairs to our more attractive drawing room. She sat upright under a portrait of Captain Scott and, between nibbles of small chocolates that she took from her bag, she spoke to me.

'I am the daughter of Ernesto de Saloman,' she said, and indeed she looked like him. She shared also his look of fear and distraction. 'I have come to London to . . .' Here she paused and attempted to gather herself.

'To find the book?'

She gave a dark smile. 'I have forfeited my right to the book,' she said. 'But there is someone else who must not have it . . .'

I am not so foolish as to think the young have no

troubles, but what could have been *so* troubling to one so young?

She attempted to reassert her proud air with a lift of her head and a little roll of her shoulders, but tears were slipping down her cheeks. She made no sound.

'I was the last to see your father alive,' I said.

She gulped and rubbed her hand angrily across her wet face.

'He spoke to me,' I continued.

Her chin was set firm, as if she were determined not to ask.

Finally she asked.

'What did he say?' Her voice sounded as if it might crack all across and shatter into a hundred pieces.

'He said he had been deceived by one he should have been able to trust,' I said quietly. 'He said that home was the last place he could keep the book.'

She suddenly turned her eyes, flooded as they were with tears, and stared at me without shame or subterfuge.

'He was right!' she burst out. 'He was betrayed, and he was killed, and . . . and . . . I . . .'

My handkerchief was clean. I passed it to her.

'It is only human to feel it is your fault when someone dies,' I said. 'If nothing else, to feel that one could have prevented it . . .'

'I killed him,' she said. 'I didn't shoot the gun, but I killed him.'

'Of course you didn't,' I murmured. 'Of course you didn't.'

'You know I did! I deceived him and I – he told you!'

There was something in her eyes beyond grief, and something in what she was saying. A slow chill of doubt crept up my spine.

'Monsieur,' she said. And she closed her eyes for a moment and she gulped. 'Monsieur, I have a brother. His name is Pierre. Pierre. I love him so much. Monsieur – he was a drug addict. Do you know about that? Do you know what it does? Monsieur, he had destroyed his health, and our family, and my heart. He was living in Paris. A month ago he came to me and he wept and he said he would go away and leave us in peace. I said no. He said he would kill himself. I said no. He said he would go to a clinic and learn how to be a human being again. I said yes. He said he owed money to the drug dealer. Masses of money. He said this man's boss would accept this book in payment. Pierre had sometimes stolen books to pay for his drugs. I stole the book, to pay for Pierre's life.'

I was silent.

'Otherwise they were going to kill him,' she whispered, so quietly I could hardly hear her.

What could I possibly say?

'You meant no harm,' I murmured. 'You were in a difficult situation. You did what you could to help your brother.'

'My father found me with the book and took it back from me. I could not pay. How could I know that these people wanted this book so much that they would kill my father? How could I know!'

'You couldn't know,' I said quietly. Poor child. Poor foolish child. She probably didn't even know that the book wasn't Mesopotamian legends, but . . . perhaps . . . Shakespeare's own diary.

When her breathing had calmed a little I said, 'Who were these people?'

'I don't know the dealer's name. I met him only once. He had a moustache, and very nice manners. Pierre had told him about the book, and he became very interested, and wanted to see it. There was someone else – the boss – who wanted to see the book. I told him I would bring it the following night at the Ritz, and he would bring the boss. But before I could meet them, my father took the book and came to London. And the man must have followed him. Or had him followed. And . . .'

She took up crying again. Crying and weeping. I put my hand on hers and she shook it off angrily.

Alas, there was nothing I could do for her.

'But the book was stolen from here,' I murmured. 'By the young boy . . .' So was the boy working for the criminal book-lover?

And Janaki was with him!

'It's true what it says in the letter,' she said. 'The book

is cursed. Despite everything . . . it brings tragedy . . .'

'Despite what?' I asked, but she just shook her head and muttered, 'If you don't know, don't ask.' She would say no more and I couldn't bring myself to press her.

'What if those people have it?' I asked. 'Would you care?'

'I would stick knives in their hearts,' she said. 'I would wish them all the ill luck that book can bring them. I have no doubt it is heading their way already.'

'The bad luck could be the police, coming to arrest them for murder,' I said. 'If, that is, you go and tell them what you have told me.'

'I am on my way there,' she said, with a grim little smile. 'I am going to lay the truth open at last.'

I offered to accompany her. Until Janaki was located, I was without purpose. I could at least escort a foreigner in mourning. As we left, I tried to condole with her on her father's death; she just looked at me from those dark eyes. I felt so sad for her that I suggested she stayed here with us until the situation became clear; and I went to bed that night very troubled indeed.

CHAPTER 21

According to Jenny Maple

Soon as I heard Mrs Lurch yell I knew what had happened. She'd been all set up for it, desperate for it. Everything was in place and soon as she got this book we'd start.

Start what? I didn't know myself. All I knew was Mrs Lurch was paying me over the odds to be there and do it, and it was indoors (mostly — apart from that trip to Mr Maggs, where it turned out we'd missed the boat), and it was clean and comfortable, and there was no police involved. All fine by me.

So 'Jenny!' she yells, up the stairs, and I come down nice and quiet like she likes me, and she's all flushed on the sofa.

'Yes, Mrs Lurch?' I respond, standing in the doorway.

'We can start tomorrow,' she says. Little rounds of red on her cheeks and it ain't the make-up and it ain't the champagne either, though lord knows she had put away enough of it last night. 'Tomorrow morning, bright and early.'

I.e., by her standards, about noon. Though to tell the truth she did look really perked up.

'There's the book,' she said. She had this smug grin on like she couldn't contain herself. She poured herself some more champagne. 'Have a drink, Jenny. Drink to my luck.'

'No thanks,' I said.

'Look,' she said. She gestured to the low table in front of her. 'That's it.'

And then she shrieked.

She had gestured to an old book on the table. What she hadn't realized was that standing on the book was seven mice. Standing, I mean, on their back legs, and giving her what can only be described as filthy looks.

Well, I shrieked too. You would.

'Go 'way!' she yelled, flapping at them. She wasn't afraid of them. The shriek had just been shock at the unexpected.

But the mice just sat there and stared.

Mrs Lurch went to pick up the book.

Now she really shrieked.

'The little graspole bit me!' she yelled. 'Call Maxim! Get him in here!'

I called Maxim.

We all stared at the mice.

Then Maxim got a broom and they ran off. Couldn't see where they went – too quick. It was all a bit odd. I never heard of no one being bit by a mouse before.

Mrs Lurch sat up late that night and put away another bottle of the Moët '36. I don't know what she was doing in there all alone. She made a phone call, telling someone that yes, she had it. She said, 'I've got it, and very little thanks to you, so you just take your pretty moustache back to Paris and – you know what? You stay on your best behaviour.' After that I heard her laughing a lot, big self-satisfied laughing, and then she was quiet for a long time. Maybe she was reading the book. Make a change. For a lady who used to be a writer – sorry, *is* a writer – she don't read much.

Tell the truth, I was a bit distracted. There was mice in the hall as well when I went through to get my supper. They was quick but I saw 'em. I was surprised. Lady as rich as Mrs Lurch, you don't expect mice, even if she is a writer.

So the next day, about noon, we go out into her dark leafy back garden like a graveyard, and we go up the twisty iron fire escape through the ivy, that I'm not to tell anyone about, and go up to the dark secret little room under the roof that I'm not to tell anyone about, and she sat me in front of the computer at the desk under the roofbeams.

I opened the book. For a moment, as I glanced at the first page, the words looked out of focus, wobbly. I blinked and squinted, and they soon came clear. Maybe I need glasses or something.

Anyway, I settled down and I started to type.

It wasn't a very long story. It was about a statue of a prince on a column and it was all covered in gold leaves, and from his column he could see all the poor people in his kingdom having a hard time, so he got this little bird to take the gold leaves to all of the poor people, only in the end the swallow died because he should have gone to Egypt in the autumn. It didn't take long to type but it was really sad.

Anyway, so then I didn't have anything to do. I didn't quite see why Mrs Lurch had got so excited about this book when all she wanted was me to copy out the story. Seemed a bit of a fuss about nothing.

Anyway, then she came back and she yelled at me and said to start again at the beginning. So I was a bit worried that she'd lost her marbles and I was being paid fifty dirhams a week just to type out the same story over and over again.

Only when I went back to the beginning, there was a different story.

And that was weird. It didn't look like some computer or something which just put out lots of different stuff. It looked like an old book of just writing, but it must have been some kind of machine I suppose, otherwise how could it have done that?

Anyway I started typing. This time the story was about a selfish giant who wouldn't let the children play in his garden but gradually he came nice and by the end of it I was nearly crying again. Mrs Lurch, however, was in a temper.

'Very funny,' she said. 'Very bliddy funny.'

'What's the matter, Mrs Lurch?' I asked. 'They're good stories, ain't they?'

'They're very good,' she spat. 'They're by Oscar Wilde. They're some of the most famous stories ever written. I want NEW ONES!'

Well, I didn't see what she expected me to do about it.

'Keep typing,' she said. 'Keep going back to the beginning.'

So I did. I typed a story about a dwarf who thought the princess liked him only she didn't really, a story about a fisherman and his soul, one about a child who came from a star, one about a student who had to get a red rose for his girl but there was only white ones so the nightingale pressed her chest against the rose's thorn and all her blood made it red, and she died singing her beautiful song, but then the girl just tossed the rose in the gutter anyway because some other young man was going to give her a diamond ring . . . I cried and cried over that one.

Then there was stories about twins lost in the woods, boys dressed as girls and girls dressed as boys, magic love potions and lovers trying to trick each other. There was one where the queen of the fairies fell in love with a bloke with a donkey head. There was one with a shipwreck, then loads about kings and queens, and murder. There was a really sad one where the son and daughter of two families that hated each other fell in love, and everybody died, and the girl was only thirteen. I cried over that one too.

Mrs Lurch came back.

'I haven't got time for this,' she muttered, angry as you like, and she sat down on the floor by the desk and propped her chin up on her fists. She got hold of the book and stared at it, as if it was the book's fault, and the book could answer her problems. Perhaps she was right. A book that has a different story in it each time – who knows what it can do?

She opened the book herself, looked at the opening page, and then threw the book on the floor in disgust.

'*The Hundred and One Dalmatians*!' she yelled. 'Are you trying to tell me something?'

I picked the book up carefully. It wasn't broken. I opened it and inside was *Jack and the Beanstalk*. Even I know that story.

'What do you want me to do, Mrs Lurch?' I asked.

'Keep typing!' she shouted. 'Skip any story you've already heard. I'll be back soon.'

So I skipped *Jack and the Beanstalk*. The next one was really good though. I didn't know if it was new or not. It was a about a rich merchant and his three daughters, and the youngest was his favourite . . .

CHAPTER 22

According to Mrs Lurch

Jack and the Beanstalk.
  The Selfish Giant.
Things were not going according to plan. It was as if
the book knew what I wanted to do and was teasing me.
Why was it giving me children's stories that everybody
knew? When it started giving me *Harry Potter*, I very
narrowly controlled my temper and sat down to think.

I needed stories to be a writer.

Sooner or later it would run out of stories that had
already been told and *have* to start providing new ones.
But when? It could go on for years at this rate.

I thought deeply.

I made some phone calls.

Perhaps we could speed up the process. A little technology, perhaps.

Then I sat down in my leather chair and read *Publishing
News*. I felt more writerly already.

There was a very interesting article about the future of
publishing: 'No More Books!' was the headline. The journalist

wrote that everything was going to be on pods and discs. Reading from paper would die out. Everything would be written in txt. Old stories would have to be translated for new generations.

I laughed.

Did my book know txt?

I thought I might buy a few publishing companies and invest in some of these new technologies. Being a writer was going to be wonderful but I have a businesswoman's heart. Once I had a never-ending supply of stories from the book, if I owned the new technology too, how very powerful I could be!

I could . . .

As I began to think seriously about it, the possibilities made me giddy. I leaned back in my leather chair. I would be able to control what stories were published and what weren't! I could destroy careers – destroy writers – by not publishing them! I could publish only my own stories, from the book! I could publish everything my father wrote!

And with the new discs and pods I could, if I felt like it, destroy books altogether.

That would serve them all right for ignoring my father, wouldn't it?

I'd start by closing my bookshops. Who needs bookshops, anyway?

I called Maxim.

What fun I was going to have. As soon as I'd got all the old stories out of the book and could start on the new ones. What fun.

CHAPTER 23

According to Lee

It was pretty clear what had happened. Bliddy Billy had nicked the book to take to Nigella Lurch and get the reward. So I had to go and get the book back o Nigella Lurch. I was scared of what might happen to him. What did Nigella Lurch want with him? Did she know about him? Did Mr de Saloman? Did Mr Maggs?

I eyed Janaki. How much *did* she know? I was pretty sure she didn't know. If you knew that a book gave out different stories, or talked, you wouldn't be able to shut up about it, and if you had to shut up about it for safety reasons you would have this air of just about bursting with the amazingness of what you know. She'd have been eyeing me with an electric look, an 'I know something incredible, do you know it too?' look. The look I was trying really hard not to have. She'd have been looking to see if *I* knew. And she hadn't been. She was still on planet normal. She didn't have a clue of what she was involved in.

'I'm hungry,' she said. 'Can I eat that stuff back there?'

We went together to look. In the cupboards under the bar were peanuts and crisps and Pringles.

'What's the sell-by date?' she said.

I passed a pot over to her. I've got loads of little tricks to cover not being able to read.

'I can't read it,' she said, and my heart skipped a beat in the second before she continued her sentence. She couldn't be illiterate. Not her – look at her! Could she? Then she continued. 'I lost my glasses when that bloke who looks like you and you won't tell me who it was even though you know pushed me down the manhole.'

It was a double whammy. Or a triple whammy, if you count my moment of confusion about whether she could read or not.

I had to cover not being able to read the sell-by date. And I had to cover the fact that it was my brother who stole the book off me.

I grinned like a sick frog.

'Er,' I said.

'So who is he?' she asked. 'You might as well tell me. I'll only keep asking and it'll drive you mad.' She had that calm girl look on her face; that 'I ain't going nowhere' look that girls get and there's no point arguing with them. She would too keep on asking.

I sort of panicked. I sort of thought if I answered one question, the other wouldn't come up. Well, I can give as many excuses as I like. I caved in at the first sign of trouble. I told her.

'My brother Billy,' I said.

She gave me a huge smile. 'That's brilliant!' she said. 'So you'll know where he'd go, and we can go and steal it back – that's really good. Brilliant.'

And to think that moments before I'd been thinking she was intelligent. How wrong can one girl be how many times in one sentence?

'Yeah, well,' I said.

'So what about those Pringles?' she asked.

Ouch.

'I can't see,' I said, holding them up and squinting at them. 'The light's bad.'

'Hold them in the light then,' she said. 'Stupid.'

I didn't like that.

'You look,' I said crossly, shoving them at her.

'I told you, I can't read,' she said, 'without my glasses.'

I was still holding them out to her, my face turned away.

She was staring at me, annoyed and slightly puzzled. 'Don't rub it in that I'm a half-blind speccie four-eyes,' she said.

I could feel that my face was completely tense.

'Joe, just read the sell-by date!'

So I pulled my arm back, and held the cardboard tube up to my eyes, and made one up.

'July 2021,' I said.

There was a pause.

'You can't read, can you?' she said cautiously.

'Yeah I can,' I said.

'Pringles were banned under the Junk Food Abolition Act of 2016, and not made again until the act was rescinded in 2035. The longest sell-by date allowed before 2016 was one year.'

'So?' I snapped.

'We did it in history. You can't read. Is it your eyes, or can you really not read? Like, you're not able to?'

I turned and stared at her straight in the face.

'None. Of. Your. Bliddy. Business,' I said, as calmly as I could, but the calm was riding on fury and shame. I picked up the Pringles and a bottle of water, and walked carefully over to a banquette as far from her as I could get, and I sat there with my back to her.

After about half an hour, she came and sat across the table from me. Her arms were full of ancient food, with their faded labels and dusty lids. She plonked them down between us.

'What do you think?' she said.

I shrugged.

'We need to eat,' she said. 'And preservatives were still legal then – so it will have lasted. I don't know . . .'

I shrugged.

'A bit couldn't harm us,' she said.

She picked up a bottle of mineral water and handed it to me. I didn't take it, so she set it down in front of me and offered me an ancient bottle of bitter lemon. Then she got stuck into the cocktail olives and saltine crackers. There were even some tiny bars of chocolate. She scrabbled one open – it had a white powdery effect all over it.

'Organic,' pointed out Janaki. 'Best leave it alone. It'll be rotten. Look – Bacardi Breezer, wonder what that is.' She twisted the top off, sniffed and took a sip.

'Yuck! Sugar on legs!' she yelled. 'How could people drink that stuff?'

The sugar she minded! It was booze, anyway.

I hate booze. Always had, always will. Seen enough of what it does. Don't like seeing people make prats of themselves and turning into sniking graspoles, to be honest. OK, some just get the giggles, but an evil drunk is an evil thing to behold and I had beheld it too sniking often. This whole place was giving me the heebie-jeebies, anyway – it's just like a temple to booze and fags. It must have been well illegal, booze and fags, in the 2020s. They were both banned then. I saw it on Discovery Channel: the Second Prohibition. Bring on the third, that's what I say.

'Don't drink it,' I said.

'Wasn't going to,' she said, and then she said, 'Listen, Joe . . .' and I closed my face again, but she carried on.

'I'm sorry,' she began to say, but I was already snapping.

'I don't need your pity thank you very much,' I said.

'I'm not sorry you can't read,' she said. 'That's none of my bliddy business, as you so rightly put it. I'm sorry called you stupid, and I'm sorry I forced you to let on when you didn't want to. That's all.'

Oh.

'All right,' I said.

Then she said she had to go to the loo.

A minute or two later she was back.

'The ceiling in the ladies had fallen in so I went to the gents,' she said. 'Look what I found.' She was holding out a small round tin with a picture of a smooth-looking bloke on the front.

'What is it?' I said.

'Hair dye!' she said. 'Well – kind of darkening oil. This was on the table by the basins. I thought you might like it, for disguise.'

This girl was doing my head in. She kept behaving like we was friends, and as far as I knew we wasn't. Not that we was enemies, but we was . . . rivals, for the same thing. She didn't seem to have noticed.

'What do you mean?' I said.

'When we go above ground. All the descriptions are about how fair you are. You could go dark. For when we go and get the book back.'

There she went again. What was this 'we'?

I had to deal with it.

'Umm – listen,' I said. 'What exactly do you think is going on here, Janaki?'

'We're going to find a way out, and go and get the book back,' she said in a tone as if she were explaining to a halfwit.

'We?' I said.

'Yes,' she replied. 'I have a right to look for it, after all, and you'll be better off if you're with me. If anyone asks you're my Scottish cousin. You're mixed race. Or maybe I am. Anyway, you're with me, and you're dark, therefore you couldn't be Joe English. So – your brother – would he take the book to this Nigella Lurch? I assume he just wants the money . . .'

Well, she was quick. Very quick. And the hair dye was a very good idea. And maybe the fact that at the end of the day she'd want to take the book back to Maggs, while I would want to keep it for my own self, was, for the moment, worth ignoring. For the moment, she could help me.

'All right,' I said. 'So, seeing as you're so clever, how do we get out?'

'Follow the Way Out signs?' she said. Pointing.

If she was going to be that bliddy clever, and that irritating, I might have to change my mind about having her along. I gave her a sarcastic look.

'But not till tomorrow,' she said. 'It's night-time remember? We'd best sleep.'

'Best to go now – fewer people to notice us,' I said, in a bid for independence.

'Let's sleep for a few hours at least, then get up while it's still dark.'

Her good sense was beginning to tire me out.

'Whatever,' I said. 'I'll take the torch and dye my hair.'

'Don't take the torch,' she squeaked.

I smiled, because she was afraid of something.

'I'll do it for you,' she said.

'No!' I squeaked automatically. No one ever touches me usually.

'I'll do a better job,' she said. 'It'll look better. Be safer.'

She was right. But I didn't want some girl's fingers in my hair.

'I'll do it,' I said, and grabbed the tin and started shovelling the gel stuff on my head.

She was laughing at me. 'Brilliant,' she said. 'You'll have one big dark splodge and your hair sticking straight up. Here . . .'

And she grabbed the pot and started doing it herself.

It felt weird. Made me think about my mother when she was nice, and that made me think about the *Beano* and that made me think about the book, and that gave me a pang in my heart. God, Billy, I hope you're being gentle with him, not banging him about. That book, with its brain and heart hidden away somewhere, that book which is so old and has been through so much, which is such a criking mystery . . . which talked to me – me! – and made itself into a *Beano* just for me even though it knew Cleopatra . . .

I was aware that this mystery was too big for one kid to deal with. I knew that other people must know about it. Something that amazing doesn't just turn up unannounced.

That's what I was afraid of. Did Nigella Lurch know what it was? I felt that she did. Why else offer all that money?

But it was me he talked to! And I promised to help him.

'Stop sighing so much,' said Janaki. 'You're wobbling about.'

My hair did, in the end, look a lot better than it would have if I'd done it. Even I could tell that.

We kipped on the dusty velvet banquettes, her on one side of the room, me on the other. Our backs were curved and our legs stuck out. There was no choice of position. I didn't think I was going to sleep at all but when she woke me at about four, I was sparko and mad. I flailed for a moment before realizing where I was and calming down.

'Take it easy,' she said. 'It's morning!'

We rinsed off in the gents, one by one, and filled our pockets with ancient peanuts.

The Way Out signs pointed along a corridor. There wa no light except for my torch. The carpet was crimson and the walls shiny cream, that's all I can tell you. There wa a reception desk with an ashtray on it.

After a while there was a double door with bars acros it. We pushed them and it opened. More corridor. Anothe set of double doors. We pushed them and they opened Some stairs up. Part of my mind was trying to work ou where we would be, compared to ground level; but I didn' know how deep Frith's Illicit was, so I had nothing to go by. I felt we were coming up, but not that we were or the surface yet. Just a hunch.

Another set of double doors with the push bars. We pushed them and they opened – a bit. But not all the way Beyond them was a wall. We squeezed and there was nc way through. All wall.

I knocked on it. Hollow. This wasn't even brick.

'What's the time?' I asked Janaki.

'Four twenty-two,' she replied, checking on her phone.

By the double door was an old-style fire extinguisher red metal, heavy.

'Wish me luck,' I said, and I grabbed it, and I heaved i straight at the wall.

With a mighty, loud and unnecessary crash the extinguishe

flew though the wall. The hole looked like a big bullet shot, jagged and spare. A quarter the force would have made it: the wall was hardly more than plasterboard.

I panted. My shoulders felt like I'd thrown my own arms through a wall – wrenched.

Janaki was looking at me, laughing.

'What?' I said crossly.

'No, it's great,' she said. 'Very macho.'

I couldn't tell if she was laughing at me or not. Anyway, she'd stuck her head through the hole.

'Storeroom!' she said. 'Looks like a deli.'

Sure enough, it was a room full of Parmesan and salami and panforte – a nice Italian grocer's. I started to drop the ancient peanuts for some better provisions, but Janaki was already heading through, looking for a way out.

'Hold up,' I said, grabbing a box of biscuits, but she was racing ahead and I followed her.

There was a door; it led to a landing. To one side, a kitchen. To the other, stairs: windy, going up. Another landing, dark wood panelling, flower arrangement on a tall desk – and a front door.

To our left we glimpsed a restaurant through a doorway, white-clothed tables laid last night for today's lunch; a coat-rack, a book for signing in. Some kind of club. Janaki struggled with the bolts on the door; I did something to the locks which I didn't want her to know I knew how to do.

In a moment we were out in the fresh air, gasping. Soho, quarter to five in the morning, a light rain, rumble of garbage trucks. I was back where I'd started, on Greek Street.

CHAPTER 24

According to Janaki

The boy was all right – for a thieving louse. Nicer manners than I'd expected and seemingly decent in his everyday behaviour. Anyway, he could help me. I don't know if I would've thought to throw the fire extinguisher, for example. And I was mortified by the reading thing. I could see it really upset him.

Out on the street we looked a little peculiar, but not too bad, for the neighbourhood. First thing, I got out my phone and checked for a signal now we were overground. But I couldn't ring Mr Maggs now. It would be inconsiderate, as he'd be sleeping.

Clearly our first stop should be an Internet cafe, where I would track Nigella Lurch and Jenny Maple.

'I'll find Jenny Maple,' he said. 'She's not the kind of girl you get on the web.'

I wasn't sure what he meant by that. If it meant splitting up, I was not in favour. What if he went off and I lost him? Well, I had the same two clues he had, and – judging by what had happened so far – a better brain with which to follow them up. But he was brave, and used to trouble, and I wasn't.

'Come with me first,' I said. 'Then we'll go and do *your* thing.' I looked a bit pleading. It worked.

The Internet search, however, did not. No sign of where Nigella Lurch lived.

We sat drinking hot chocolate in the all-night Internet cafe, the lights bright and the mood peculiar. My mouth had a nasty taste in it from the earliness of the hour, and the hot chocolate was so fake that it did not help.

'You could come back to Maggs with me,' I said suddenly.

He looked surprised. I was surprised myself.

'I have to let Mr Maggs know that I'm all right,' I said. 'If I tell him you're trustworthy, he'll trust you.'

I could see the words on the tip of his tongue: 'But I'm not trustworthy.' He didn't say it.

I didn't trust him, anyway. But I wasn't convinced he was a bad guy at heart. And I wanted to keep him close. What's that saying – 'Keep your friends close, and your enemies closer'?

'Come on,' I said. 'We can have baths, and bacon and eggs, and you'll be safe from the police.'

I think it was the bacon and eggs that swung it.

We walked there, down little streets, him nervous and quick, me tired but exhilarated. He did look very different with the dark hair, but I could see he didn't want to stay visible for long. Also, it occurred to me that *he* might not trust me! Which of course from his point of view was perfectly reasonable.

It gave me something else to think about though, as we scurried through the dawn light. Was I going to hand him over to the police, in the end?

After a while, I said, 'Don't worry. Really, it'll be all right. Please trust us. We're trusting you, after all.'

He looked at me with his silvery-blue eyes – too light to be real – and I did my best to look friendly and innocent. I had no intention of betraying him. He and his brother just wanted the money; I just wanted to get the book back. That was all.

To be honest, he looked like an animal at the end of a chase. He looked like he had nowhere else to go.

'Where's your mum?' I asked him suddenly.

'Where's yours!' he responded rudely.

That shut both of us up.

When we were nearly at Berkeley Square he paused for a moment and got out his phone.

I pretended not to listen.

'Finn?' he said.

Whoever it was was clearly asleep.

'No, don't say a word. Don't tell no one I called. All right? Schtum, Finn. I need to know where Judy M is. That's all. You on your own? What? Oh. Oh, really. All right, get me the address then. He's what? He's there, is he . . . Oh, crike . . . Finn, don't talk to me about Billy. I don't care what he does. Listen, if he wants to end up a drunk like Dad then . . . What? How would I know where he got the caio? How much has he got? What are you suggesting, Finn? No! I told you before . . . Yeah . . . Well, just don't say you've talked to me . . . Listen, it's not my problem, Finn. Yes. I know. Poor Mum. If you don't like it or if Mum doesn't like it then why don't you run away too, yeah, and live on the streets and have no caio and nowhere to bliddy go – yeah. Finn – you know about Dad and me. You know I ain't talking to him ever. You lot have got to look after Mum. It ain't safe for me to try – Oh, Finn, listen, man. I can't do nothing. It ain't worth the aggro, Finn – Listen, just get me that address. I'll call you later. Yeah, man. Sorry.'

He ignored me after that. His tight little face was as white as a piece of fish.

I walked on ahead like I hadn't overheard any of it, but my mind was ticking over it and I was very curious.

So Billy had money – which meant he'd handed the book over already. And Joe was telling the truth about the hard time and the tough home life.

For a moment, I thought of my father. I didn't even know where he was. To be honest, with Mama dead it makes no difference. I was most concerned to do the right thing by Mr Maggs.

I had a tiny, half-formed, wispy memory of Mama

Perhaps it was not even a memory, but an imagining, or a memory of an imagining. It is a feeling more than anything. A feeling of warmth, a sense of smooth flesh, a brown cheek, a strand of smooth hair, a curve, a sweetness. Perhaps I made it up. It makes me cry when I think of it.

I, who had lost my family, wondered what it would be like to choose to leave your family. How dreadfully he must have suffered, to choose to leave. How could that feel?

Like his pale face, I supposed. Pinched and tight, for the rest of your life.

I walked quicker. I wanted Mr Maggs and the smell of old books.

And then it struck me.

If Billy already had the money, why was Joe still here? Why didn't he just go and argue with Billy? He didn't need to go to Nigella's . . . He didn't have to give me the address. He didn't have to help me.

I was alone, and I was stuck, and I had nothing to go on, and I was out on the street at dawn. And I had failed.

All I could do was call the police, but if Nigella Lurch has the book and she'd offered the reward and that was all legal, then . . . It just didn't seem right. Mr de Saloman had left it with us. My head was whirling.

'So, you'll be off now, I suppose,' I said.

'What?' he replied.

I might as well ask. I had nothing to lose.

'Well, if Billy's got the money, you don't need the book any more . . . I was wondering, would you . . .?' There was no reason why he should but maybe he would. 'If you get that address, would you tell me anyway?'

'The money? I don't give a toot about the money,' he said.

I was shocked. I'd thought . . .

'Then what . . .?' I said.

'It's the book,' he said. And then a look of shock passed over him, as if he realized he'd said something impossible. Which of course he had.

'But you can't read,' I said. 'What do you want the book for, if you can't read?'

He was staring at me, his face as unreadable to me as the book must be to him.

He couldn't answer the question.

'I just do,' he said. It was a pathetic answer.

'Joe,' I said, 'tell me the truth. I'm an honest person and I need the truth.'

At that, he laughed. 'Yeah,' he said. 'You wouldn't believe it.' And that was all I got out of him. But as we walked along, my brain was ticking over and over all I knew about this peculiar book, and I was deeply puzzled.

Soon enough we were home. I led Joe through the back entrance, took him upstairs to bathe and gave him a pair of my jeans and a shirt to wear. Couldn't help with the shoes of course. The fuss he made about the shirt, you'd think he'd prefer to wear clothes covered in sewage.

Mr Maggs wasn't up and Finn rang back within the hour. There was an address in Hampstead. I could see Joe thinking about going off without me. I had, however, taken the precaution of double-locking the doors. I mentioned it to him. Along with how good a likeness that picture of him in the paper had been. He got the message.

'Come on,' said Joe, as soon as he'd polished off three eggs, six rashers of bacon, two cups of tea with three sugars in and an extraordinarily large amount of orange juice. 'No need to hang about.'

So we didn't.

I left Mr Maggs a note, of course.

Dear Mr Maggs,
    I've found Joe English and we're going now to get the book back.
    In haste,
    All well,
    Janaki

Joe rolled his eyes, but I felt sorry for him. Imagine having no one to leave a note for.

CHAPTER 25

The Story Continues According to Finn Raven

I was really really narked at Lee. Really narked. First he's telling me porkies, saying he hasn't got this book and he don't know nothing about it; then he's bossing me about, telling me not to tell Dad this and not to tell Billy that, and then he's ringing me in the middle of the night requiring information.

It wasn't that I'd been asleep. Fat chance, round our house. It's only little where we live, and Dad and Billy got no idea about night and day. I have to get up, because I have to go to school. They're really tough on me about that, what with Lee and everything. Dad says he can't afford the fines. Mum just goes wet-eyed. So usually I go.

Anyway, Dad had been out all night again. He and Billy only come in about a half-hour before Lee rang me. Dad was in a grand mood for a change.

'Liza!' he's yelling. 'Come and fix me my tea! Where's tea for your best boys!' He was shouting and bumping into stuff, but not in that bad way, so I just went back under the pillow. Mum had to get up and get them something to eat. He called it his tea but it was nearer breakfast.

I could hear him in the kitchen, slobbering his drink and stuffing his face.

'What's perked you up then?' Mum asked.

Billy and him were laughing in a secretive way, like only they knew something really brilliant and they hadn't made up their minds yet whether to share it. I know that laugh.

I snuck out of bed, managing not to wake Squidge, who was snoring through it all as usual. There's a place by the kitchen door where I can stand to listen and not be seen. I didn't want to be seen. Dad's mood can turn so quickly sometimes, and then it's all yelling and throwing stuff and Mum crying, and when that happens I don't want to be there. Lee used to always try to get Dad to stop, trying to protect Mum, but it never made no difference. Just made Dad turn on Lee. And then Mum'd be cross with him too, saying he shouldn't get involved.

Anyway, none of that tonight. It was all laughing and joshing, and Dad saying, 'Young Billy's in the money, Liza, that's what. Our little layabout's done good, is what. Go on, Billy, dash yer mum a bit of caio. Lay out the tosh.'

I peered through the crack of the door.

Billy, his face all red, was grinning away and laying out piles of cash on the table. Big piles. Hundreds of dirhams. Thousands. I could feel my eyes going big.

'Billy,' says Dad, 'found a valuable item and traded it in.

He got the reward, didn't he? And that's not all he found! Guess what, Liza!'

Mum was giving the smile she always gives him. The 'please don't start I'll be really good just don't start' smile.

'He found our Lee!' said Dad. Something in his voice reminded me of a crocodile. 'Guess where our Lee was, Liza?'

Mum was going water-eyed. She always did when Lee was mentioned – so we didn't mention him. Except Dad, who didn't care about people crying.

'He was down the Tyburn at Stratford Place, Liza,' grinned Dad. 'And you know what?'

Suddenly I knew what was coming.

I was right.

'HE HAD FULL KIT! HE HAD THE BOOTS AND THE MASK AND THE TORCH AND THE WHOLE CRIKING LOT! HE HAD FOOD!!! HE HAD EVERYTHING HE COULD NEED FOR A COSY LIFE BELOW! FINN!!! COME IN HERE AND EXPLAIN TO YOUR MOTHER WHERE HE GOT IT!!!!'

His hand snaked round the door, grabbed the collar of my T-shirt and dragged me into the kitchen.

'Where'd he get it, Finn?' he said, quietly now, with a deadly smile.

I was shaking. I know it's pathetic but when my dad

shouts I go to pieces. I'd say anything. I'd tell a million lies or anybody's secrets. I know it's pathetic. It's just my dad. He's like that.

He was staring at me now, his eyes all watery and blue, and the veiny cheeks. He was fat but he was strong.

'I took 'em,' I said. I felt I was going to wet myself.

'And did yer tell us, Finn?'

'No, Dad,' I whispered.

'Even though we're out of pocket every day he's off school, paying them fines, and it's breaking your mother's heart?'

'Yes, Dad,' I whispered. 'No, Dad.' I didn't know what he wanted me to say, I didn't understand what he was saying even. I'd just give him yes and no and hope I got it right. He panicked me.

'And where is he now, Finn?'

'Don't know, Dad,' I whispered.

'Where was he when yer last saw him, Finn?'

Mum was washing up — one cup, over and over, with quick jerky movements. She had her back to us. Billy was leaning back on the two back legs of his chair.

I gave a weak sick broken sort of cowardly smile.

'He went up the Tyburn, didn't he, Finn? He got in at Bruton Lane, didn't he, Finn? So what was he doing down Berkeley Square? Billy here tells me he was at Maggs the Booksellers. I might just go down there later and see what's going on. Shall I do that, Finn?'

'Good idea, Dad,' said Billy. 'We could all go.'

I was just grinning my stupid weak grin.

So Dad gave me a nasty clout over the head and told me to bog off back to bed.

Mum was still staring at the sink. Her shoulders looked all soft.

So when Lee called I was under the covers, feeling small.

I asked Jenny's mum later about Jenny, and I was glad Lee was going to where she was because that meant he wouldn't be at Maggs if Dad did decide to go there. I may be narked with Lee but I wouldn't wish Dad on anybody. And Dad's angriest of all with Lee, because Lee got away.

But anyway, Dad had fallen asleep, and when he falls asleep after a late night he doesn't wake till dark usually. I'll just have to be out.

CHAPTER 26

According to Lee

Jenny, bless her, had told her mum where she was going to be staying, and told her not to tell anybody. Her mum, bless her, had always had a soft spot for Finn (loads of mums do, crike knows why) and she told him, and told him not to tell anybody. Jenny, she told him, was doing a spot of work for a lady writer up in Hampstead and had to live in. She was staying with the lady writer and every day she had to go to a secret bit of the house up a fire escape in the back garden with all dead leaves and spiders.

So we just went up there. The house was on a corner, dark and tall; the windows shuttered. The gardens front and back were walled, and full of dark heavy trees with the kinds of leaves that never fall off, just get dirtier and dirtier over the years. The earth under the trees was dry and hard and grey. A few acid-coloured new leaves, curling and warping at the ends of grey branches, were the nearest to spring that sprouted in this dark den. Janaki and I staked the house out for a bit to see who came and went. Answer: not a bliddy soul.

Nobody came, and nobody went. And then after a while Jenny came out of the front door and went down the side of the house by the street wall. A few minutes later there was a shaking and rustling in the thick creeper growing up the back of the house. I nipped along the street to get a better view.

In among the dirty leaves I thought I caught glimpses of human leg and of dark iron railing.

OK.

Along the street, on the next corner, was a first-floor cafe. I had clocked it earlier. From its back room, sitting at the window table, we could see the front door and garden wall of the house.

We sat quietly drinking tea, watching the door.

'Well,' I said, 'I'll go in later and if it's there, I'll have it back.'

'I'm coming too,' she said.

'No, you're not,' I replied.

'I am,' she said.

'You're not,' I replied.

We could have gone on all day but I thought I'd shut her up. 'Burglar alarms,' I said. 'Do you know how to avoid them?'

'No,' she said.

'That's why you're not coming.'

She stared at me with those big brown eyes.

'If you steal that book back and then make off with it,

she said seriously, 'I will come after you and make you sorry.'

'Course you will, darling,' I said. 'You and the entire SAS. Abseiling.'

'Just watch me,' she said, and batted her eyelashes at me and picked up a copy of the *Beano* that she'd been reading, and began to giggle at Dennis the Menace.

Yeah, well. I just sat and watched across the road.

It was a long day.

Around one o'clock Jenny reappeared from the back of the house. She appeared on the side street – no doubt she had let herself out of a back garden door. I'd check that later. She came down the street in our direction, swinging her arms and hopping a bit from foot to foot. It was amazing how innocent she looked. She didn't look old enough to have keys. Then she disappeared from view.

Until she appeared in the caff, up at the counter, ordering herself a sandwich. I grabbed Janaki's *Beano* and held it up in front of my face. I didn't think Jenny would recognize me, but you never know. I was kind of scrunched down, head to the window. Janaki was squinting at me. She was just the type who, instead of recognizing a crisis, would say really loudly, 'Why've you taken my *Beano*? Are you trying to hide from someone?' So I kicked her under the table.

Jenny didn't look round. She was in a world of her own.

So much the better. She took her sandwich and went downstairs and back to the house. She went down the side street again, and then there was the rustling in the greenery again. All right then. I knew the route. The only question was security. It might, I realized, be better to go in while Jenny was there and the security was off. Which would be easier to handle – a girl or a millionaire's security system? No question.

An hour or so later, a woman appeared at the front door and I nearly had a heart attack.

It was Romana Asteriosy. I'd know her anywhere. Dripping with fur coat, strutting little manner. She had enormous sunglasses on now, otherwise she looked just how she'd looked that night in Soho. She had the same handbag. She was taking keys out of it and double-locking the door behind her.

Why was Romana Asteriosy double-locking Nigella Lurch's front door?

I thought furiously. What was the connection between those two?

Why did Nigella Lurch, who hadn't had a book published in six years, live in a millionaire Munster mansion? And how come, actually, she had 25,000 dirhams to offer up as a reward?

Romana Asteriosy was coming out on to the street. She walked right under our window – I could have spat on her dyed blonde head. Pray god she's not coming in the cafe too. I felt my scalp prickle beneath my dyed black hair.

On the main street she hailed an electrocab and climbed into it.

'Is that her?' said Janaki, gazing out of the window over my shoulder.

'Yeah . . .' I said slowly.

'And?' she continued.

'And what?'

'And why do you look like you've seen a ghost?'

I leaned back in my seat, rolled my shoulders and smiled.

'Because I think I have,' I said.

'What?'

'Tell you later,' I said. 'I've a house to break first. See you, sweetheart.' I chucked Janaki annoyingly under the chin.

'See you, darling,' she said, even more annoyingly.

The back garden door was heavy with rivets and gleaming locks. It took me two seconds to scrabble up the dusty ivy and leap the wall instead. As I crouched briefly on the top, I noticed Janaki in the street behind me. I glanced down and she gave me a little wave.

'I'll be waiting,' she cooed quietly.

I was too busy lowering myself invisibly into the garden to tick her off. Later.

I couldn't see any sign of CCTV or detector beams, but you never know. Usually they wouldn't be used in a London garden by daylight – every squirrel or feral hoglet would set them off. Even so I used the basic avoidance technique, I'd known all my life. (No, I can't tell you what they are. Course I can't.) I slipped along to the back wall of the house. The foot of the fire escape was well hidden in a big twisted lump of undergrowth, but I could see where Jenny had trampled leaves to get there and I found it easily.

Up the rusty iron stairs, fighting hairy loops of tough old ivy and scratchy rose branches all the way. Keeping my movements small. Heart pounding. I was, by this stage, very curious. My blood was up. I was full of questions but I just wanted to get hold of the book and keep it safe.

I wondered if the book knew I was coming. If he could sense me. 'I'm coming,' I whispered. 'I'll manage . . . I'm coming.'

At the top, a tiny balcony and a wooden door. An open wooden door. A low, whizzing, mechanical noise was going on inside: quite quiet, repetitive, regular.

That's when I heard the squeaking.

The little blighters were right at my feet. Rodents. Well I had enough of rodents down the shores. Don't like rodents anyway, tell the truth. There were seven of them In a row across the entrance

A straight row.

Looking at me and going nowhere.

I stared at them.

They stared at me, as if judging me.

Then they ran, in their straight row, one after another, into the ivy and they were gone.

Most peculiar. What the crike that was about I didn't know.

I returned to the door.

I stepped through it silently, looking around.

Jenny was there at a desk. She turned and looked up.

Clearly I wasn't as silent as I'd thought.

I smiled at her.

'Jenny,' I said, 'don't say a word. You know who I am, don't you?'

She nodded, dumb with fear.

'Jenny,' I continued, 'you say nothing and you do nothing. All right? Else Billy, and Squidge, and Finn, and Ciaran, and my dad, Jenny – yeah, my dad – will come round and see you. And your mum, Jenny.'

She was nodding desperately.

'Understand?'

Nod nod nod.

Sometimes it is useful to belong to a notorious bad family.

All right then.

And then I turned to see what that noise was, from the other end of the little room, and what I saw made my blood feel as if it had turned into something else. Some cold liquid metal, lurching in my veins.

I don't know what I'd expected.

I'd kind of worked out what Nigella might be up to. What would a writer want, after all, with a book that produced new stories all the time? It don't take Einstein to work that out. Particularly when she wasn't any good.

But I hadn't expected this.

There stood a tall heavy glass box like a display cabinet, metal-framed, lit from above and below. Inside it was the book. It was open. Too open. Its pages were flattened like it was being pinned back. The spine was crunched up behind . . . It looked painful.

It had been put on something that looked like a sharp metal spider. Some of the legs held it firmly and the others were flicking over its pages, fast like a deck of cards in the hands of a magician, flicking through the whole lot then slamming the whole lot to the back again and starting over. It was as if somebody brutal and inhumanly quick was reading the book, over and over, incredibly fast.

It was clear to me how much this hurt him.

There was a kind of screen close up in front. Greyish, underwater-coloured, glowing, it stared at the pages as they flickered past and emitted low, pulsing flashes.

The light was cold and ghostly. The noise continued. The regular whirr and slap. I thought of racks for stretching heretics; of dungeons where prisoners were held in irons, hanging from the wall. Limp and broken. Like that guy the book had told me about who had given fire to mankind, and he had to lie stretched out and tied down on a mountaintop forever, and an eagle came every day to eat his liver.

It reminded me of something else too. Photobooths. Photocopiers. *Scanners.*

The book, it seemed quite clear, was in some kind of torture machine. He was being held prisoner, and he was being copied.

I crept up close and I looked at my friend, locked in the glass machine. The pages went at such speed that it was nothing but a blur.

'Booko!' I called out. 'Booko, mate, I'm here! Can you hear me? I'm going to get you out! Hold on, all right!' Could he hear me? Did he know I was here even?

I hadn't noticed at first a computer screen attached to the back of the machine. I looked at it. Pressed the up button. Pages and pages of writing. Pages and pages and pages.

The stories were spewing out the back on paper. I picked up a page as it flew out. Black squiggles on white. Meant nothing to me.

I didn't have to be able to read to know what was going on here. This machine was stripping stories out of the book. Harvesting them like fruit, ripping them out like diamonds from a mine, dragging them up like a huge trawl net.

I had never seen anything more wrong in my life.

I pressed my mouth against the glass.

'Don't worry,' I whispered. 'I'll help you.'

Behind the whirr and slap I thought I heard a thin, sad noise. A moan.

Well, it was obvious really. Turn the bliddy machine off.

I couldn't find the plug. It was all built-in, encased in rubberized plastic. I didn't want to cut through anything, set everything on fire. Right, have to turn off the electricity where it came in.

Sheets of paper were still spitting out. I glanced at one and thought, *Those squiggles aren't right. Look, it's the same one over and over again.* And as I did a voice behind me snapped out, 'Who the hell are you? Stand up and step away from the scanner!'

Well, it was her – Romana Asteriosy. Up close she looked like a film star who'd been inflated with a bicycle pump. Still had boiled meat for a face though underneath.

'You're hurting it,' I said. 'Turn it off.'

'What?' She clearly couldn't believe my cheek but couldn't give a toss about that.

'You're hurting the book,' I said. 'Turn off your stupid machine. A book's not a factory – look, you're exhausting it.'

I held out the piece of paper in my hand.

She looked at it. 'Jesus,' she said, and turned to the control panel and pressed a few buttons.

The whirring stopped. The flicking stopped. The paper stopped shooting out of the back of the machine. The last page fell, and settled.

It was a moan I heard. It tore my heart.

She flicked another switch and the front of the case slid open. I was already there – before she turned around I was in there, lifting the book gently from its torture frame, closing it, cradling it in my arms.

'It's just the machine,' she said. 'There's something wrong with the scanner. The book's all right.'

'No, it's not, you stupid jerk,' I said. My breath was going hard. Where before I had felt the life of the book when I held it, now I felt weakness, tiredness, old age. It was dry and limp. There was no strong breath of life in it. 'You've used it up. Just stripping the heart out of it – what the hell did you think you were doing?'

'Give it to me,' she said, but the look in my eye must have scared her because then she said, 'Show it to me.'

I wasn't even going to bliddy open it. I held it close to my chest, safe in my arms, and surrounded it with everything in me that was warm and alive. I was murmuring to it under my breath, 'I've got you. Don't be scared. I'll look after you.' There were tears of anger in my eyes as I stared at this stupid woman.

'Let me look,' she said. She'd put on a sweet tone o voice.

I swore at her, calculating how to get past her to th door. I could kick her, if need be, but I couldn't fight he off with my hands while I was holding the book.

She frowned and rubbed her nose.

'Listen,' she said. 'We just need to see if it's all right Come on, just open it.'

'All right? What, all right so you can keep on exploiting it and working it to death?'

'Let's just see . . .' she said.

I stared her right in the face. Gave her my iciest, pales look.

'You,' I said, 'go over there. I will look at the book here And if you move, I'll break your jaw.' I was taking a risk She could have a securityguy on his way now.

She swallowed, then moved across in to the room t where I'd gestured.

I went towards the door and gently put the book o Jenny's small desk there. Jenny shifted away, still rigid lik a rabbit before a fox.

Tenderly, I opened it.

The pages were blank.

Ah – well, they would be, for me.

I stroked the opening page gently. No Dennis th Menace? No lions?

'You,' I called. 'Jenny. Have a look at this.'

Jenny peered over at the page.

Nothing.

'You – Mrs whoever you are, whatever you call yourself. Come over here. And if you make one move I don't like, I'll deck you. Don't think I'd mind decking a bird. It'd be a pleasure, since it's you.'

She came over – delicately. I'd scared her all right. No doubt she was working out in her mind how to call her security, but by my judgement she hadn't called any yet.

'Look,' I said.

She looked down at the open pages. Nothing.

I stared down. Please, please, let something appear. Please.

Nothing.

Not a single illegible black squiggle emerged on that empty white page.

We waited far longer than was likely. Hoping.

Nothing.

'Well,' I said in the end. 'Bravo. You've done what thou
sands of years of history have failed to do. You've killec
it.'

'No,' she said, and to do her credit she did look upset
'No.'

'Well, yeah, actually,' I said.

She sat down, as if her knees had buckled.

Jenny stood there goggling.

'You stupid disgusting greedy woman,' I said, and, taking
the book into my arms again, I turned on my heel anc
scarpered.

CHAPTER 27

According to Janaki

When that film-star-looking woman came back and let herself into the back garden she closed the door behind her and I was stuck there. There was nothing I could do.

So ten minutes later, when Joe reappeared over the wall, breathless and with high spots of colour in each cheek, I was still there at the door.

He was clutching the book and setting off at a run.

'You've got it!' I cried, taking off after him. 'Fantastic! Oh, brilliant! What happened? I thought when that woman turned up – there was no way I could warn you, Joe, I'm sorry . . .' I was really looking forward to getting a look at it, finally.

But his face was not a face of glory and success. He was nearly crying, and he was hurtling and stumbling. I raced alongside him.

'Joe? What's the matter?'

'My name's not Joe,' he said. And he kept striding on. Behind me I heard a door slam.

He glanced back and put on speed. Up the hill and then over towards the main road. I was panting already.

'Joe!' I yelled.

Footsteps behind us.

I couldn't keep up with him.

Joe disappeared round the corner.

A tall blond man was gaining on us.

It was one of those do-or-die, who's-side-are-you-on moments. I didn't hesitate. I just stuck my foot out and tripped him. The noise when he hit the pavement was quite unpleasant, but not as bad as his language.

'I'm so sorry,' I said. 'What a speed you were going! Can I help you up? Dreadfully clumsy . . .'

He stared at me and brushed himself down. He looked at the crossroads. He swore. I smiled politely.

'Well, if you're quite all right,' I said, and strolled on. Behind me the woman and the girl appeared. It was the girl who had come to Maggs. The woman started shouting at the blond guy.

Tra la la. I just walked on up the hill. The moment was round the corner I hailed an electrocab, jumped in and followed the road Joe had taken. He hadn't got far.

'Pull over a moment,' I said to the cabbie.

'Joe!' I called. 'Come on – they think they've lost you.'

He got into the cab. All his cockiness was gone. All his cheek and know-all attitude. He slumped in the corner and there were tears on his face.

'Where to then?' asked the cabbie.

'Just keep on,' I said. 'Joe – where shall we go? We should get back to Maggs . . .'

At that he turned on me. 'I'm not going to bliddy Maggs. Now crike off and leave me alone.'

I sat quietly, just looking at him and thinking calmness. Calm, calm, calm. I tried to send it right inside him.

'Maggs,' he said.

'Yes,' I said.

'Do they mend books and all?'

'That's exactly what we do,' I said. 'Buy them, sell them, store them, look after them, mend them, rebind them . . .'

A tiny flicker of hope appeared on his icy face. Then it faded again.

'I can't,' he whispered. 'He'll tell the police . . . They think I had something to do with that murder.'

'He won't tell . . .' I began to say, then I realized that I couldn't promise that at all. Mr Maggs might well tell.

'And they'll take the book back . . .' he was murmuring.

'Well, you've got to go somewhere,' said the cabbie. 'Or will I drop you off here?'

Joe's face was desperate. He flung his head back and he looked like he was dead.

Then he lifted his face. 'Take us to Cromer,' he said.

'Cromer?' said the cabbie. 'You feeling all right? That's 200 miles, and forty miles into the Drowned Lands.'

'Course it is,' said Joe. 'Sorry – I was just thinking about my auntie. How much to take us to – oh – somewhere on the edge of the Drowned Lands? Anywhere.'

'The road's all right as far as Norwich,' the cabbie said with a little laugh. 'I'll take you to Norwich for a hundred.' He quite clearly didn't think we had five dirhams between us.

Joe smiled and produced a roll of cash from his pocket. 'Fifty now,' he said, 'and here's the fifty for when we get there.' Then he turned to me. 'We'll drop you at the station,' he said.

'Oh no, you won't,' I replied. 'I'm coming with you.' We argued about it almost as far as Cambridge.

CHAPTER 28

According to Lee

So I was sitting there in the back of the electrocab, just holding the book, up to my neck in misery. I thought if I held him, my warmth, my life, might seep into him and give him strength. He had learned to talk when I needed him to! So I would somehow give him what he needed.

What did he need?

He needed to rest and be loved. He needed to tell stories. He needed to tell them to human beings, who would laugh and cry and be interested – not to a machine.

He needed to be read. Well, I couldn't read him. I couldn't learn to read . . . Could I? I –

Crike, but my head ached.

But even though I couldn't read him, that didn't mean I didn't want the stories. He knew that. So I sat in the back of the electrocab, holding him safe in my arms and telling him, quietly, how much I wanted to hear the rest, when he was ready.

Janaki was giving me some strange looks, it's true. I wasn't bothered.

She leaned forward and turned off the speakerphone to the driver's cab.

'Joe,' she said in important tones.

'My name ain't Joe.' I'd told her before.

'What is your name?'

'Lee,' I said.

'Lee. Oh. OK. Lee, why are you talking to the book?' She asked it in a very tender voice, like I was a halfwit or a moody two-year-old or something.

'Mind your own sniking business,' I said.

She did, for a little while. Then she started up again.

'Lee,' she said.

'Yeah?'

'Why did you call yourself Joe?'

'So you wouldn't know who I was,' I said.

'Why?'

'Mind your own sniking business,' I said.

So then she snuckled back in the seat a bit and took to just looking at me sideways.

I didn't have the energy to make her go away, so I let her stay. She wanted the book, I wanted the book – so what, the book wasn't going anywhere till it was well again. If it got well again. I was so done in, to tell the truth, that I didn't care if she was there or not.

And she had been all right so far. Kicking Nigella's bloke!

Ah yes, Nigella. Or Romana.

It was the same woman, no doubt about it. Nigella, the authoress who'd disappeared off the face of the earth, and Romana, the crooked mastermind who'd appeared out of nowhere – and maybe wanted to go back to nowhere again – with the book.

But this was more than just a never-ending supply of stories for a lazy author. If she'd wanted to do that she wouldn't have needed that evil machine. She could have just – you know – copied them out. What was she after?

Some time after Cambridge Janaki dropped off. I felt like dropping off myself, after the night we'd had. But I carried on murmuring to the book, concentrating on him, comforting him, loving him.

For a while he just lay, light and dry, still and strange. You remember what I said earlier about holding an animal or a baby when they're sleeping? The book wasn't asleep.

He was sick. So so sick.

I kept on murmuring, wanting, hoping, needing.

I don't know how long it was. We were just driving on and on. Trundle trundle trundle.

It must have been great when there were petrol cars, when the motorways were new and had no potholes, and people could go a hundred miles in an hour. Now we had to stop every hour to juice up, and the driver kept muttering about not ruining his suspension for a couple of daft kids. Tall forests of wind turbines glided by beside the road, some of them ankle-deep in water. At the juice-stops I pulled my hood round me and pretended to be asleep.

After a long long while, I gently opened him again. His spine was stiff and rasping to the touch. I held him carefully, only opened him a little way.

And a tiny voice drifted out. So feeble – a tiny little voice like Granddad Fred's when he was in the hospital with his emphysema.

He said, 'Oh, Lee.'

Crike, if he'd been human I would have given him such a hug!

'Booko!' I whispered intensely. 'Booko! Talk to me, man. You all right?'

'No,' he said. 'I'm . . . Thank you, Lee.'

'S'all right, mate,' I said. I was embarrassed suddenly.

'You saved me,' he murmured.

'Hope so,' I said.

'You did,' he murmured. 'Not since I was kidnapped by the storm god Zu have I been so well rescued . . . You came after me and got me. You said you'd look after me and you did . . .'

'S'all right,' I said again, whispering, holding him. 'Is it OK to be open? It doesn't hurt you?'

'It's fine,' he said. 'Stay with me.'

'Ain't going nowhere, man.'

I tucked him into my jacket, next to my heart, where he'd be warm. And as I did so, I looked up to find Janaki's big eyes just goggling at me.

'It's talking,' she said.

'What? What's talking?' I said automatically.

'That book,' she said. Staring.

'Book? Talking? What you on about?'

She wasn't falling for that.

'Stop it,' she said. 'I just heard that book talking to you and you were talking to it. It said, "Stay with me", and you said you weren't going anywhere.'

Well, she was bound to find out sooner or later.

'OK, yeah,' I said. 'And if you ever mention it to anybody, ever, I will cut your tongue out and sell it for salami down Leather Lane Market.'

'I don't think you will,' she said. 'You're not the type. But don't worry, I won't tell.' She looked a bit green.

'Hey, take it easy,' I said. 'You want the window open?'

She did. She breathed deeply out of it for a few moments. Then she turned back to me.

'Joe,' she said. 'Lee, what is it?' She was talking in a kind of frozen way. Shock.

'It's a book with peculiar powers,' I said gently. 'It's something quite amazing, actually. But I ain't going to tell you that much about it because it's secret, if you see what I mean . . .'

'And Mr de Saloman was murdered because of it . . Oh, my days, I have to ring Mr Maggs . . .'

'No, you don't,' I said. 'And that is why I ain't going to tell you anything else. You got what we call divided loyalties, and I only got room for one set of loyalties, which is – the book. That bliddy woman just nearly killed it. You didn't see what I saw, Janaki . . .'

'I wouldn't do anything to hurt the book,' she declared. 'Ever. Nor would Mr Maggs. I promise you. He could help. He knows about books . . .'

'Not this one,' I hissed.

The cabbie was pulling over.

I shot Janaki a shut-it look and turned on the speaker-phone.

'We there then?' I asked.

'Yup,' he said. 'Cathedral do you? Station?'

'High street,' I said.

We'd need some supplies for where we were headed.

CHAPTER 29

Mrs Lurch

That boy. That dreadful dirty thieving little guttersnipe. That he could just walk in and help himself to my book, after all that I have been through to get it, and in my hour of glory he just marches into my house, ignoring my security, threatening my sta , tricking me, and then just gets away with it . . . The back garden is meant to be secure. Maxim is meant to monitor the CCTV. Jenny is meant to have a tiny spot of intelligence – enough to press the panic button you'd think. But no. Nothing. He walks in, insults me and jumps o over the wall, and Maxim falls over while chasing him. For crike sake, this would never have happened in Russia. We could have just shot him. My compound in Moscow was surrounded by landmines and everybody knew it. You don't get many burglars then, I can tell you. But here they still have all these stupid laws.

God, I'm fed up with being outside the law. A quiet life is all I want. A nice quiet life like I had when I was Nigella – that's all I want. Country home. Dogs. My marvellous new business. First I would be Queen of Books, and then I would single-handedly destroy books, clearing the way for a new and brilliant future! The name of Lurch would no longer be just that of a poor unpublished author and his sad little family . . .

And now that boy, that filthy little white-faced child, has . . . Oh, I could spit.

That Joe English. Oh, I knew it was him. That ludicrous hair dye didn't fool me. He stole my purse and now he has stolen my book.

I couldn't go to the police. The last thing I needed now was a connection to be made in public between Nigella, whose book had been stolen, and Romana, who had been robbed of her purse. Romana was the past and Nigella was to be a new clean future. As far as the police knew, Nigella had made her offer of a reward and that was it. I couldn't exactly tell them I had acquired it by other means and lost it again.

This took my thought back to the young man who had brought it round and to whom I had paid all that money.

How had he got his hands on the book? How had it got from Maggs to him? Who was he?

I pictured him in my mind and another question rose quietly up.

Why did he look so like the young thief who was making my life hell?

I sat quietly, and I thought, and I thought, and I thought.

And then I decided to take a step back in this puzzle. I would go and see Mr Edward Maggs.

CHAPTER 30

Mr Maggs

Eliane was drinking hot chocolate on the roof. I took this as a good sign. She had been so thin and unhappy, and surely chocolate and the view out over the cherry blossom of London would cheer her up. I was desperate for news of Janaki and to know that at least one of the young women for whom I felt responsible was all right made me feel a little better about that.

She had told the police everything. She told them about the drug dealers in Paris and they said they would look into it. I had told them about the boy who had stolen the book. They said they would look into it. Sergeant Foley was very kind and helpful. And then he came back and told us that the police were at a loss. None of these leads led anywhere. He was frustrated about it. He was very sorry. There were hundreds of drug dealers in Paris. He couldn't really go and ask them all if they or their bosses were interested in old books, could he? Nobody knew who had killed her father. It was, they said, a professional job – as if a gangster had done it, or an army hitman. No clues at all. He had been shot, the gun had been found in the lake with no fingerprints. They had been unable to trace it. Its manufacture numbers had been filed off; it had never been registered anywhere, no ID chip, nothing. There were no witnesses other than the person who had heard the cry of 'Eliane!' in the night. And the boy thief couldn't be found.

And that was it.

I went and joined her in the evening sunshine. She was sitting on the lead tiles, looking out over the park where her father had died.

'Monsieur Maggs?' she said.

'Yes, my dear.'

'Where is the book now?'

'With the boy who took it.'

'Monsieur Maggs . . .?'

'Yes?'

'My father left it with you because he trusted you. I leave it with you also. I think I know he left it to me in his will – but I do not want that book. It has made too much pain in my family. But one thing I ask you.'

'What, my dear?'

'Do not sell it. Do not let anyone have it for money. This writer who says my father give it to her – she is lying. Do not let her have it. Do not sell it. Keep it quiet and safe. Only if somebody understands it let them see it. It is a strong and strange thing. I cannot tell you all that it might be . . . Keep it safe.'

I wondered if the grief had disturbed her sanity. But she seemed quite rational, apart from on the subject of the book.

'But – Eliane . . .' I said. 'My dear – as you have raised the subject, please allow me to . . . Eliane, your father told me the book contained Mesopotamian legends. But when I looked at it . . .'

She turned to me and smiled. 'It contained something else?'

'Yes,' I said. 'I haven't mentioned this to anyone because I had no time to confirm my hopes . . . but why would your father say that what looks very like Shakespeare's diaries were Mesopotamian legends? Why did he tell me this story about not being allowed to look inside? What *is* all this about a family curse?'

'Shakespeare's diaries? Oh!' And she began to laugh.

'What!' I demanded. 'What's so funny?'

'Oh, monsieur.' She said. 'Oh, I am sorry. Oh, my lord. Well.' She sighed. 'Monsieur, I will have to tell you. Yes. I wasn't going to, but I have thought it through and if you are to keep the book, if we ever get it back, then you need to know. We are not in the Middle Ages now.' She looked at me closely. 'You would never have the patience and obedience my father had. I will tell you what I found out simply because I was a naughty curious little girl who on one occasion did what she had been told not to do and opened a book she had been forbidden to open. Then you will understand exactly how desperate I was – desperate – to save my brother. You will know why I am to blame for my father's death. And you will know what you are dealing with.'

And she told me. How the book, each time you go back to the beginning, has a new story in it. How as a girl she would sneak to it when her parents were out, and read and read and read. How as she grew older the stories grew with her. How they were always right for her mood and the moment. As if the book knew what it was giving her each time.

I couldn't quite understand what she was saying and made a stupid answer.

'So it's not Shakespeare's diary?' I said.

'Shakespeare's diary is what it knew you would like,' she said.

'How right it was,' I murmured. I was keenly disappointed. But at the same time, my god! My god, what a thing! If it is real, my god!!

'And where is it from? What is its history? Such a thing must have made itself known before . . .'

'I don't know,' she said. 'It had been in the family for many years, but before me the instruction not to open it was respected.' She shrugged her shoulders. 'I don't know where we got it from.'

But as she spoke, I realized that I knew something of it myself.

The Book of Nebo. The old legends.

I must ring the British Museum immediately – somebody in the Mesopotamian department would be able to tell me all about it.

Oh, my days . . .

That was when the doorbell rang. I jumped up and rushed down the stairs. Perhaps it was news of Janaki!

It was a very over-made-up young woman.

'Mr Maggs,' she said, smiling, 'I do hope I'm not disturbing you. I am Nigella Lurch, the authoress. May I come in?'

Perhaps she knew something. Cautiously, I led her into my study.

'I am so concerned about the lack of progress by the police in poor Ernesto's murder,' she said. 'I was wondering if you had heard anything.'

'Nothing,' I said truthfully.

She didn't seem to know that Eliane de Saloman was here. I wondered if she even knew that Eliane existed. I wondered if she had ever even met Mr de Saloman. I wondered – and then it hit me.

She knew the book's secret.

Why else would a total stranger claim to have been given an old book by a murdered man? Why else would she offer this great reward?

She knew what the book was.

She was looking at me now, bright and smiley. Lying toad.

'And of course the book he so kindly gave me before he died . . .' she said. 'I suppose you haven't heard anything . . . since it was stolen . . .' I knew what she was getting at. Since it was stolen *from here*, implying it was all my fault. Her property, and my fault. Well, it was my fault it had been stolen, but it wasn't her book, or her business.

Perhaps she had murdered him! Or had him murdered!

I would tell Sergeant Foley.

Oh. Tell him what – that the book is an ancient mythological book with magic powers? I can imagine what he would say to that! No. But I would tell him she desperately wanted it and should be investigated.

I smiled at her.

'I'm afraid I have heard nothing at all, Ms Lurch,' I said. 'Have you?'

'No,' she said, smiling back at me.

And that was it.

After she left, I rang Janaki's mobile number again. I wished I had paid more attention when she had taught me how to text. I would have used any method I could to get in touch with her. It had been nearly twenty-four hours since I heard from her and I was worried sick.

CHAPTER 31

Janaki

So there we were in Norwich, drinking tea in a cafe again, armed with food, water, sleeping bags, wellies and a couple of waterproofs. Lee seemed to have plenty of money. Lord knows where he got it from. He'd found a special waterproof bag for the book as well, and wrapped it in it, and tucked it back inside his jacket.

'Where are we going, Lee?' I asked at last. I'd been desperate to ask since we got in the cab.

'We're walking,' he said.

'Walking where?' I asked cautiously.

I could see he didn't want to tell me.

'We're walking east,' he said finally.

East!

'East is the Drowned Lands,' I said. 'The border is right here. We're not allowed. It's dangerous. All washed away, remember? Perilous swamps and sea currents? What are you talking about? We'll never get through and if we do we'll drown too. The quicksand'll get us. There's nothing there anyway. Why do you want to go there? Don't be crazy. Don't you mean west?'

No wonder he hadn't wanted to tell me.

'You can go back if you want,' he said, cool as you like.

'No,' I replied firmly. 'Just explain to me what's going on. Where we're going.'

'If you want to come with me,' he said, 'you'll have to trust me.'

I looked at him.

'You're full of ultimata, aren't you?' I said. 'Bossy. All right. I'll just go to the loo and then I'll follow you blindly into god only knows what.'

So I went to the bathroom and I got out my phone. I'd been keeping it turned off. I didn't want to remind Lee that I had independent connection to the rest of the world. He was so touchy . . . but now, finally, I was able to speak to Mr Maggs.

He was so relieved to hear my voice and at the sound of his I began to realize what a desperate situation I was in.

'Mr Maggs,' I said, when he had calmed down a bit, 'listen, I'm all right. I'm with Joe English, only his name is Lee Raven, and he's all right . . .'

At this Mr Maggs huffed and puffed a bit.

'No, I'm pretty sure he's all right. He's got some bad habits but he has a good heart – trust me, Mr Maggs. He has the book – it was damaged –'

Here he gave me three minutes on why we should've brought it back to the shop for mending.

'Lee is very attached to the book, Mr Maggs. Nigella Lurch got hold of it somehow, and it was damaged, and Lee now just wants to . . .'

How could I explain this without letting on what the book was?

Then Mr Maggs said, 'How much do you know about the book, Janaki?'

Ah. He knew all about it then.

'I know,' I said. 'I know it is . . . special.'

'He must bring it back,' he said. 'Please. Persuade him.'

'He thinks the police are after him for Mr de Saloman's murder. He won't come.'

'Where are you?'

'We're – we're in Norwich. We're going into the Drowned Lands.'

There was a horrified silence.

'Why are you doing that?' he said at last, and his voice drew smaller and tighter.

I was so ashamed to worry him like this. I had to sound confident – far more confident than I felt – to reassure him.

'It's his plan,' I said. 'He seems to think he knows what he's doing – Listen, I have to go. I'm taking too long, he'll get suspicious. I'll ring you again. I –'

I couldn't do it. I rang off. I didn't want him to hear me cry.

Oh, lord, what was I doing? Was I doing the right thing?

I heard in my mind again the book saying, 'Stay with me', and Lee saying, 'I ain't going nowhere.' I *know* he's not a bad boy.

I can't let him go off alone with the book. They both need me. And I am carrying the honour of the House of Maggs.

And then we left the cafe, and once we were out of town we pulled on our kit, and we walked and walked till the road suddenly disappeared from beneath our feet, to be replaced by a salty dark swirl of shallow sea water.

The great dark eastern sea, the drowning sea, spread out before us, shallow, treacherous and cold. Beneath it, washed away by it, undermined by it, still bravely sticking up through it, were the remains of East Anglia: the cities and fields, cathedrals and houses, farms and factories, the broads and beaches.

'High tide,' Lee murmured. 'Head north.'

I followed him. The wind off the sea was keen, and I pulled my coat collar round me and tucked in my scarf, but even so it slid cold fingers down inside my clothes. We were walking on long scrubby rough grass, the kind that cuts your legs when it whips against them, leaving the long rolling waves to our right.

It grew darker. There was a small moon, high and solid in the clouds. The going was tough. I was shivering and sweaty at the same time. Night-time drew in and I walked on through it.

After about a mile and half, Lee suddenly said, 'Here we go!'

I nearly tripped over it. Something solid and rough in the reeds. It was a boat.

'No,' I said.

'Yes,' said he.

'But where are we going?'

I was terrified. No way was I getting in that tiny boat to go out on this treacherous sea, with all the ruins of the old towns and villages under the shallow water, bits of them sticking up, sharp, at night, in this wind, by moon-light, with a thieving boy . . .

'Janaki,' he said, and for the first time he touched me. He put his hands on my shoulders. 'Look at me,' he said. I couldn't see him anyway. The clouds were scudding over the moon in tatters.

'I am not putting you at risk the way you think. I wouldn't do that to myself and I wouldn't do it to the book. Just shut up and we'll get on with it. We're going in the boat, not very far. I know where we're going. All right?'

It wasn't all right by a long chalk. But there didn't seem to be any choice.

The water eddied and swirled around my feet as I

climbed into the little boat. Lee got the oars. They were locked up but he seemed to have a key for the padlock. This reassured me – up to a point.

Almost as soon as we pushed off, the sea wanted to befuddle and thwart us, sending us this way and that with contradictory currents and waves. Lee took the oars and handled it. He found a path. He rowed us – straight out from the low, vulnerable land.

He seemed to know where he was going. The sea grew calmer. He was counting strokes, and changing course from time to time, and listening to the sounds of the sea. Once or twice he touched the bottom with his oar and pushed us off again like a gondolier. I sat in the stern, shaking with fear, clutching my coat around me, shoulders hunched and jaw tense.

After about twenty minutes he said to me, 'Do you see a shadow to the left?'

I looked. Left was north. Shadow? It was all shadow. I couldn't even make out the horizon where the dark sea met the dark sky.

And then I did. Darker on the dark sea, I saw several. Some were low. Some were sharper, larger and angular. One seemed to have arms, stretching out. Behind them all loomed a great ring, standing high in the night sky, a silhouette of starlessness. A shaft of moonlight shone on it and I saw it was a real thing, something solid. Further over, something was flapping.

I heard a high distant creaking.

Lee pulled the boat round and headed towards the low, looming shadows.

I bit my lip.

One of them was drawing really very near.

And when he rowed us right into it, I screamed out loud.

'Shut up,' he said, and rowed us through a big hole, an entrance of some kind, as if into a cave. The darkness became much smaller around us. The moon disappeared. And Lee pulled the boat over, and fumbled, and anchored it.

CHAPTER 32

Lee

We spent the night in our sleeping bags, in the boat, anchored inside the old concrete skating pipe. Not exactly comfortable. Ate some biscuits. Got some kip. It was all right.

First light woke us. A few shady fingers of grey came in the entrance at each end. Crike but it was cold. Janaki stirred, and sat up, and burst into tears.

Looking around at the slimy concrete and the dull grey expanse beyond, I can't say I blamed her.

'Come on,' I said. 'Sun'll be up soon. It'll warm up. We'll straighten things out.'

I got up, stretching out my cramped and twisted legs. The water was about a foot deep, flat and sheltered. I pulled on my wellies.

'Come on,' I said. 'We'll find a gaff and I'll dry some weed and we can have a fire . . .'

That livened her up. 'A fire? We're in the middle of the sea. How are we going to have a fire?' But she sat up, and scratched her head wildly so her hair all stood out, and she asked for a bottle of water.

I waded out and climbed up the concrete steps on to the roof, and looked out over our peculiar haven and its mad landscape. Soon enough, she joined me.

'Oh, my days,' she said, staring around her. 'What is it?'

All around us were the skeletons of giant machinery, up to their knees in long rolling sea. Huge rusted hulks, collapsed or lurching in the seabed, still rooted in their twentieth-century concrete, but ravaged by twenty-first-century sea levels. You might think they were scaffolds and cranes and terraces from sports grounds, reduced to their iron frames, but for the last remnants of tattered and faded decoration and revelry that still hung from them. A tall round twisting structure had a few painted candy stripes just visible at the top, where the water hadn't battered it quite so much. A framework like a great frozen octopus, legs awry, still had a little pointy boat hanging from one or two of its limbs, a spaceship perhaps, with a shiny number 8 on it. A couple of other spaceships lay nose first in the water underneath it, where they had crashlanded. Barnacles clung to their rusted upturned bottoms. A huge flapping sign hung down from a crane arm, green and yellow remains of a flowery design in its corners, and the blackened stubs of a hundred missing light bulbs studding the edges. From the great geometric circle, still towering above the rest, small cabs hung and creaked in the sea breeze. All it needed was little human skeletons in them, shrieking and waving and losing their caps and popcorn.

'It's a funfair,' she said.

'Yep,' I said.

'It's weird.'

'Yep.'

'Is it safe?'

'Nope,' I said. 'That's why we're here. It is extremely dangerous. Imminent collapse, etc. Nobody in their right mind would come here. Look at those signs.'

The wide chain perimeter fence which we'd negotiated the night before was strung with metal signs reading 'No Entry', 'Danger of Death', 'Toxic Area' and suchlike encouraging phrases. Some of them might be true. But as far as I knew nobody had come to any harm here.

Over to the left were the remains of a fortified hut where a security guard had been lodged, years ago when some company had plans for the ruin – plans which came to nothing. The hut, however, remained. I had high hopes of the hut.

'Let's go and have a look,' I said, pointing it out to her. 'It's either that, or the skatepipe, or the old Ghost Train.'

The hut had a dead seal in it. Complete with maggots and god knows what eating it, and a stink as revolting as the shores.

'Ghost Train it is then,' said Janaki. I think the daylight cheered her up.

We slopped away on foot past the Flying Saucers and under the Big Wheel.

She stared up at it.

'It could fall, couldn't it?' she said.

'Pigs could fly,' I said. 'Looks all right to me for now.' I kicked it and a shower of salty rust flakes fluttered down on our heads.

The Ghost Train tunnel was water-filled ankle-deep, like everywhere. The air became denser and smelly: dank, metallic, salty – like engine oil and canvas and mould. The roof was low and dim, tattered with dangling remnants of lord knows what that had been hung there to frighten the daylights out of the children of fifty years ago.

But part of the works was housed in a chamber above the tunnel – it was the bit where the skeletons were concealed before they jumped down on you. This little room was above the water level, so it was dry and nice. Well, drier and nicer. Plus it had a hatch at the side, facing towards land. This could be our window and lookout spot. Not that I was expecting anybody. But you never know.

The machinery which had worked the skeletons was a bit in the way, and the wooden skeletons themselves were swollen with the damp air and stuck in peculiar positions, but we found that if we whacked them and folded them over they made quite good chairs.

'I'll go and get the boat,' I said. Janaki was getting the

window open, rattling it and pushing. 'If you can get some of that thick grey weed, it'll burn when it's dry.'

When I got back, she was sitting under the window, her head in her hands. I took off my boots, started unpacking the little stuff we had, and offered her an apple and a bit of salami for breakfast.

We sat on the skeletons and munched. For the first time I felt relaxed.

'Lee,' she said.

Crike, her and her questions.

'What?' I said.

'How did you know about this place?'

I grinned. 'My great-aunt Jobisca,' I said. 'She used to ride the Wall of Death on a motorcycle here when she was young. Years and years ago. She told me about it.'

'But that was before . . .'

'Not really,' I said. 'Norfolk and Suffolk having been falling into the sea for centuries . . .'

'Yeah, but before this part was drowned . . . What about the boat?'

'Family stuff,' I said, but she gave me such a look that I continued. 'It's a bolthole for Ravens. If any of us is ever in trouble, we can come here. It's safe, because everyone else thinks it's dangerous. Aunt Jobisca knew how it was built – her husband's granddad did the concrete and he was the best. She paid a guy in King's Lynn to keep the boat in good nick. It's here for us, if we need it.'

'So does your dad know about it?' she asked.

'Course not!' I said. 'It's him we'd most likely be running away from!'

The sun had moved round and was coming in the hatch now. Janaki turned her face up to it.

'Well, we can't stay here forever,' she said.

'Nope,' I agreed. 'But we can stay here for now.'

She got out the bedding and laid it in the sun to air. Then she lay down on it and went back to sleep.

Me? I took out the book, and sat it in the sun, and opened it up.

'You all right?' I enquired.

'Not bad,' he said. He sounded sleepy.

'Do you like the sun?' I asked.

'I love it,' he said, so I laid him on my belly in a pool of sunlight.

After a while, quietly and gently, he began to tell me about a boy who stowed away on a pirate ship.

A while after that, I saw that though Janaki's eyes were still shut, she was awake, and she was listening, and her mouth was smiling.

I don't know if the book noticed.

It's really inconvenient him not having a face. How can he be so like a person but not have a face? There's so much you can't know . . . He's so mysterious.

CHAPTER 33

Nigella

Well. How very naive nice people are.

It took me one minute to talk my way into Mr Maggs study and one minute while his back was turned to fix my little bug on to his telephone.

And not much longer for the girl to ring up and tell Mr Maggs – and me – all we needed to know.

The Drowned Lands!

What an intelligent place to take a valuable, indeed irreplaceable, book.

I'd better go along and bring it back.

Maxim!

CHAPTER 34

Lee

Looking back, I really liked our time at the fair. Seems weird, because we weren't that comfortable and it was cold and damp and we weren't safe and we knew we'd have to move on . . . but it was nice.

First thing, we prepared our defences. We collected stones, bits of metal, crocks of concrete, anything we could find, and we lugged them up the Big Wheel to the top. Was it hard? Yes, it was. Climbing a rusty old pile of machinery with a sack of rocks on your back is hard. The first part was OK because there was a set of metal maintenance steps built into the main trunk of the wheel, but after that we had to clamber up one of the arms at an angle, and then round the frame to get to the bit holding the cab on, and then let ourselves down into the cab itself. We mangled our hands and broke our nails and stubbed our toes and strained our muscles reaching from one rough girder to another, always afraid that something might shift in this giant rusted-solid Meccano, and tear our flesh, or drop on us. But in the end we had two cabs armed with enough ammo to give a decent battle to anyone who might turn up after us. I also, though Janaki didn't know this, had a packet of flares, two catapults and four strong fine-weave fishing nets that I'd got in Norwich. I put the nets and catapults in the cabs too, tucked away under the seats, along with most of the flares and boxes of matches. A couple I kept on me. I wasn't expecting anybody but you never know.

Janaki dried seaweed in the sun. I went out in the boat a few times and caught fish. The night we made a fire for the first time, and cooked three little mackerels, was really nice. She was laughing at my jokes, and she sang me a song in her dad's language and I laughed at that. We ate the hot food and had a cup of hot tea. It don't half make a difference, hot food and drink. Especially when you're living like a frog, in and out of the water.

So we were sitting with our tea, and she said, 'Lee – do you think – do you think the book would, um, tell us a story?'

Well, I had been thinking about this. Now that Janaki knew about him, and knew he spoke, would he speak to her?

He was getting better, that I knew. We'd had a long chat that morning while Janaki went on a half-hour walk – well, wade – to try to find somewhere private to pee (yeah, like I'd be looking at her!). He was still weak, but he was getting better.

But would he speak to me with her there? Would he speak to her? I didn't know. And I didn't want to be cheeky and assume anything. And I didn't want to ask him, in case he felt obliged . . .

'If you open him,' I said, 'he'll tell you what he needs you to know.'

Her eyes lit up.

'May I?' she asked.

'Of course,' I said. 'He's here for everyone to read.'

So I carefully handed him over, and I saw how gently she held him, and how carefully she turned him over to look at his vellum cover, and how tenderly she finally opened him.

She started to read.

'What's he say?' I asked almost immediately.
Tell the truth, I was jealous. She was doing the thing he was for. I couldn't do it. I felt left out and a bit useless. But I wasn't going to be angry with her about it. Not her fault I can't read. I can't go on being angry with everyone else about that.

'It's from the Bible,' she said. 'It's the bit where Jesus says, "Render therefore unto Caesar the things which are Caesar's".'

'What's that about then?' I asked. Bible study is not my strong point.

'It means, I think, that everybody gets what is right for them, and you don't get what is not yours. So I suppose he means he's not going to speak to me because that's not right for me, for some mysterious reason. Oh well.'

She was disappointed.

And a bit cross.

'Why does he speak to you then!' she burst out. 'What's so special about you!'

Well, that made me laugh.

'I ain't special!' I cried. 'He talks to me *because* I ain't special. He talks to me because I'm useless.'

'What?' she said.

'He talks to me because I can't read him.'

'What?' she said again, being pretty dim for a clever bird.

'I can't read, Janaki. Remember? I can't read. I am illiterate. So the book tells me stories instead. And through telling stories, we got chatting. And through chatting, we got friendly.'

Her face was a picture.

Me, I felt kind of good. Just saying it out loud.

She looked down at the book, which lay there all silent and innocent in her hands.

'So he's like a person,' she said.

'Yup, in many ways he is.'

'And I'm holding him.'

'Yup.'

'Can he hear us?'

'Course he can.'

She stared at him for a bit, taking that in. Then she gulped and said, 'Doesn't he think it's a bit familiar, me holding him and him hearing and thinking and everything, and not saying anything to me, and me not able to see his face or anything? Has he got a brain?'

'He's a mystery,' I said. 'That's the point.'

'And isn't it a bit rude of us to be talking about him in front of him like this?'

'I don't know,' I said. 'I think he must be used to it.'

And then she held the book up in front of her face and she said to it, 'I'm sorry if we're being rude. It's just even if you're used to it we're not. Well, I'm not. So I'm sorry, I didn't mean to rude.'

And the book said, 'Well, that's all right, dear. I understand.'

And then I was really jealous.

He didn't say anything else to her. Or me. He went back into silence. So did I. I just quietly took the book back off her and said, 'I'm going to sleep now. Night.' I still had that headache, to tell the truth, and all this damp and bad sleep wasn't making it any better.

The next morning I felt I had been snarky, so I let her read him. It was good for him to be read by her. I knew it would make him stronger. She was a good reader, just the kind he wanted, clever and interested and full of passion. She didn't talk to him again, and he didn't talk to her either.

Maybe I had been mean. It wasn't like I was in charge of him, anyway. He could talk to whoever he wanted, if he wanted.

When she went off to pee again (I just peed out the window. Girls are funny though) I opened him up.

'Did I hurt your feelings?' he said.

'Bit,' I mumbled.

'You saved my life and I would do anything for you,' he said. 'You gave me my voice and, if you like, in your life-time I will speak only to you.'

'Nah,' I said. 'I ain't in charge of you.'

'Do you trust Janaki?' he asked.

'Yeah,' I said. 'I think I do. I think she'd always want to do the right thing, so I couldn't be much of a scamp round her. Like she wouldn't sit by and let me nick stuff, but I think she'd be loyal.'

'I think so too,' said the book. 'And you, are you prepared?'

'What for?'

'For the future, Lee. For the challenge ahead.'

'Nope,' I said, in all honesty. 'I can escape though. I'm good at that . . .'

'Yes, I've noticed,' he murmured.

'. . . but I don't always know what else to do.'

'Lee,' he said, 'this is the end of running. It's time to face your enemies.'

I heard a noise – a distant rumble.

I turned. Looked out the hatch.

Oh, holy crike. A speedboat, roaring towards us in a blur of spray.

Who the crike knew where we were?

I thrust the book inside my jacket.

Where was Janaki?

I nipped down the Ghost Train, barging through the last remaining dangling cobwebs. I peeked out the end.

The speedboat noise was droning and straining. I moved my head round a little and I could see it – they wouldn't be able to see me though. It was about 500 yards away. And it wasn't moving. It seemed to have run aground.

Well, thank crike for that.

There were two people on board. They were fiddling with the engine. One was waving their arms.

I didn't have much time.

I dodged behind the Octopus and headed for the Big Wheel. Janaki would know to join me there as soon as she noticed the boat. But would she notice it in time?

I couldn't help her.

They were engrossed in their engine and didn't see me as I snagged round to the back of the Big Wheel. I was halfway up the maintenance steps when I spotted Janaki.

She'd seen the boat and was coming round the back of the skatepipe. I didn't think she could see me, but it looked like she was heading for the Big Wheel.

I headed on up, keeping myself as best I could invisible

against the girders. The morning light was behind me, so that was in my favour.

I'd made it to the wheel frame when I spotted Janaki on the trunk below me. She glanced up and I gave her a tiny wave of encouragement. She waved back and carried on climbing.

The figures from the boat had given up and were starting to wade towards the fair. One I could make out was a woman. Blonde. Oh yeah. The other was holding something out in front of him, like a gun.

All right then.

How the crike had they known we were here? I lay flat against the iron strut, muscles aching, getting my breath back, and I listened. Their low voices did carry over the water, but I couldn't make anything out.

Below, Janaki was gaining on me.

If they didn't spot us before they were close enough, we had a chance.

They were staring at the water, picking their way carefully.

I twisted, arched and slid down into the cab. Crouched there, I kept my head low. The weight of my landing had jerked the cab into movement. Pray they wouldn't spot it.

After a couple of minutes I peeked over the side. They were still picking their way across, nearing the skatepipe now. Janaki was on the wheel rim, edging towards me.

Looking up at her there now, I saw how exposed she was, how far it was to the shallow water below, how hard and horrible the metal around her was. Grimly she shuffled along, her body flattened for invisibility. She was heading to the cab beyond mine – why hadn't I gone to the further one when I had the chance and left this one free for her. Now she had further to go, at a more dangerous stage.

My head was pounding again and I felt hot.

Something rustled at my feet. I glanced down. A rodent!

Now how in crike did a rodent get here?

Never mind that now. The man and woman – I could see them quite clearly now – were poking around the skatepipe. Presumably they'd find the boat.

Sure enough. The man was dragging it out.

And kicking a hole in it. Well, that's nice. So there was our transport, scuttled.

The woman quite clearly didn't like being in the water. She didn't even seem to have wellies on. It's amazing really how dim people can be. How do you get to be a mysterious gangster queen, clever enough to find out where we were and not be bright enough to put on a pair of wellies?

OK now.

Janaki was above my head now. I wanted to call out to her, but instead just turned my head up and gave her a big grin and a thumb's-up. She grinned back at me and wriggled on. In a moment she was lowering herself into the cab, and dangling there about three yards away from me, way up in the sky.

The intruders were approaching the Ghost Train.

They didn't go in – just peered through the entrance and then moved on.

Towards the Big Wheel.

Janaki and I glanced across to each other. I held up a flare. She smiled, reached down and held up a flare. I held up a box of matches. She did the same. Stones, catapults, all in place. We had planned to start with stones.

They were in range beneath us. The first blast would be the only one with the element of surprise. We each had a bag of stones and we each lifted them.

Eye contact.

Another grin.

A lovely feeling came over me in that moment. It was like she was my brother and we were together against the world, doing the right thing.

I really liked it. I liked her. It felt good.

Five, four, three, two, one.

GO!

We each leaned over the edge of our cab, and we tipped and tossed the whole barrage down on their heads. Not stopping to see what damage we'd done, we loaded our catapults and began to fire alternately, big stones, aimed at them as they scurried away from the wheel. We had to fire accurately. We didn't want to just scare them out of range. We wanted to scare them away completely, or damage them.

Janaki kept firing, covering me while I peered over the edge of my cab.

The man was down! He had blood on his forehead and was on his knees. For a second I felt a pang at having hurt him – but then sheer anger took over. It was self-defence wasn't it? I didn't ask him to come after us with a gun. Then another stone hit his back. The combination of cata-pult and height made the hit strong. He buckled and went on his face in the sea.

The woman, her hands up around her face for protec-tion, splashed across to him and turned him over. The water was just too deep. I could almost see her thinking what to do – drag him somewhere and prop him up? Or give up on him and leave him to drown?

Janaki hit her right in the belly. Crike, this girl is ruthless!

Nigella made her decision. She deserted him.

Splashing like a wild thing at a watering hole, she launched herself towards the main stem of the wheel where she would be sheltered from our missiles. Was she intending to climb up? I imagined her standing down there back to the rusty iron, catching her breath and realizing it was two against one.

Janaki stopped the onslaught.

The silence settled.

And I caught the sound of a voice – Nigella's voice – floating up. She was on the telephone.

Reinforcements!

I craned and craned to hear what she was saying. Couldn't make it out. No idea how far away they were, or what the plan was.

I glanced across at Janaki. She had her mobile out. She made a questioning gesture – as if to say, shall I ring for help too?

'Who?' I mouthed.

'Mr Maggs!' she called back, low-voiced, intense.

Fat lot of good he would be! She understood my body language clearly.

'Police?'

How to do 'Janaki, I am wanted for bliddy murder, no don't call the criking police!' in sign language?

She shrugged. Could I think of anyone?

No, I couldn't.

Finn?

What could Finn do?

I couldn't think of anything or anyone I could turn to.

And that's when I saw the helicopter.

At the same moment Janaki squeaked and cried, 'Lee! Look!!'

She was pointing out to sea. Out to sea, where we had not been looking, for obvious reasons, was a boat.

I laughed. Great. And I caught her eye and I pointed

out the helicopter. It was a long way away and it was heading directly towards us.

She took a deep breath and blew it out.

Beneath us, Nigella began to climb the steps.

And, deep in my jacket, I heard a voice.

'For god's sake, Lee, let me out.'

'Don't be daft,' I said. 'I'm suspended in a little swing on a wrecked Big Wheel hundreds of feet in the air above the sea, with enemies coming from three directions, and any minute now I'm going to start bombarding them with fireworks. Now is not the time for a story.'

And he said – it was the first time he'd talked without me opening him, but I suppose drastic times call for drastic measures – he said, 'Child. Which of us has survived thousands of years, the siege of Nineveh, the sacking of Alexandria, the Reformation, and other dramas too many to mention? Stop wasting time. Take me out and put me on the seat.'

'No!' I said. 'I have to keep you safe!'

And then I began to feel a warmth, a burning sensation against my chest where the book lay, and a throbbing against my heart, and the book spoke again, and he said in thunderous tones, 'Do as you are told!'

So I did.

I opened my jacket.

I didn't even have a chance to put the book down – he burst out, filling the space in front of me, growing before my eyes, massive, changing, not a book at all, a great – a great –

A figure.

A man.

A man with big eyes and curly hair, muscular, tall, bearded, wearing pale clothes and a determined look.

He turned to me. 'My face,' he said. The familiar voice. 'My brain,' he said, pointing at his head. 'My heart,' he said, and he tapped his chest. 'Me,' he said. 'My eyes, my mouth. My hands.' He waggled them. They were huge. 'All right?' he said.

I was blinking and croaking.

'Battle, Lee,' he said. 'Are the flares for the helicopter? Good. They'll distract it.'

And then he whistled, and called out, 'Mushusshu! Daughters of Mushusshu!' and then I had to sit down, because all around me were mice, lining up, and they were shivering and as they shivered their skins seemed to fall away from them, and without their skins they grew a little and shook themselves out, and I was surrounded by tiny dragons, the size of kittens, with long wings and sharp teeth, dancing and bowing around him in a frenzy of delight. They were incredibly beautiful. They shone and shimmered. They also seemed to be singing. I held on to my head.

From the other cab, I heard a matching croak of human amazement. I looked over at Janaki. She was staring.

'Did you know about this?' she mouthed.

'Not a criking clue,' I said.

The dragons' dance of delight was swift and soon they had gathered round him as he – who was he? – spoke to them low in a strange language.

He glanced up and broke off for a moment to say to me, 'Nebo. Call me Nebo.' And for a moment he smiled and it was as if the sun had come out on my entire life and then he turned back to his dragons.

Nebo.

'He says to call him Nebo,' I called to Janaki, as if in a trance.

She nodded slowly.

With a raised finger he dismissed the tiny dragons and they rose in a cloud. For a second they hovered and then they poured over the edge of the cab in a gleaming purple green and silver stream, down towards the sea.

A moment later there was a shriek.

The dragons reappeared. Their wings were blurred with speed as they hovered in a row in front of the cab. Suspended from their diamond-sharp claws like sagging laundry from a line, by her clothes and her flesh and her hair, was Nigella Lurch. She was squawking with terror and indignation.

'Woman!' said Nebo, and his voice was ringing and magnificent. 'You ridiculous person! I am not yours and never will be! I am not for sale! Money does not buy me Greed does not win the fruits I can give! Do no more harm out of your desire for me! Do not attach your idle fantasies to me!'

And with that the dragons dropped her. Just like that.

We heard a splashy thud and a final squawk. But they were drowned by something more immediate.

'The helicopter!' I shouted.

The sound was roaring up on us now. Janaki and I grabbed our flares and matches.

'May I help?' said Nebo, and he took one too.

I grinned at him.

The copter hummed towards us. I could see figures through the windscreen. I could see a gun carriage at the side. I could see the copter turning, leaning, to position itself. And I could see two gun barrels aiming right at me. It's not a nice sight.

'NOW! NOW!!!' I yelled, and we let them off, straight at the great domed windscreen.

Janaki was already reaching for another flare – but the deed was done. All three hit. The screen was shattered. The gun shot uselessly into the air as the copter twirled idly on itself for a moment, then with a huge creaking twist it lowered its head and fell in a great tumble to the sea. The dragons circled it curiously, as if it were a giant of their own race, a great fallen beast. And it lay in the shallows, surf ruffling its belly, its rotors still swinging slowly.

Now there was only the boat from the sea to deal with. I turned to check. It was still a long way off. As the helicopter's moan subsided, there was quiet. My ears were ringing.

Nebo sat down.

'Come here,' he said.

There wasn't far to go, just across the little fairground boat, but I went and I stood near him.

He took my hand. Warm strength emanated from him.

'All right?' he said.

I nodded. Couldn't speak, to tell the truth.

'Good,' he said. Then he glanced across at Janaki, raised his eyebrows at her, and turned back to me.

His eyes were golden brown. His hair was greying at the temples. His face was lined and tough and tired. He smelt like honey and oranges. He opened his arms, and he hugged me, and I put my arms around him, and I felt the warmth and the strength.

'I'm not really meant to do this,' he said. 'The *Beano* is one thing, but human form is quite another . . . but you wanted it so much. And I have to give people what they want. No one else ever wanted it.' He looked down at me. 'Thank you,' he said, and rolled his shoulders in the breeze and took a deep breath. He looked out over the Drowned Lands. 'What a beautiful world,' he said. 'Enjoy it.' And he tweaked my cheek, and then . . .

And then . . . then the book lay in my hands, warm and heavy.

I was surrounded by tiny dragons, weeping.

'The boat, Lee!' yelled Janaki.

I swiftly turned to aim a flare at it, but pulled myself up.

Someone was jumping up and down on the deck, waving his arms and shouting.

'Lee! Lee!' he was calling.

It was Billy.

He jumped overboard and came running like an elephant through the surf. 'What the crike's all this?' he yelled up, his voice lifting and scattering in the breeze. 'You all right, man? What's been going . . .? Great shot . . . helicopter! Bliddy marvellous! It's all over then . . . what? Who . . . bloke? You sure . . . all right?'

I started laughing. Or crying. Or both.

I put my hand over the book. Stroked it for a moment, then put it back in my jacket and tucked it carefully in.

'Shall we?' I called to Janaki.

'Er, yeah,' she said. 'Yes. We'll go down. Yes.' She looked like she'd been winded. Which she had, in a way. Both of us had.

The climb down took a long time. For some reason we were without strength, dazed and confused, and without confidence in our ability to climb. I felt very weak. We were very careful. Little mice scurried down around us, and we were careful not to put our hands on them, or knock them off.

Billy, at the bottom, greeted me with a massive hug.

'Man, oh, man,' he said. 'That was something. Bringing down that copter. Man, oh, man. Hey, gorgeous,' he said to Janaki, then he ran over to look at the helicopter. couldn't bring myself to.

'Dead as doornails,' he reported back. 'The pilot and the other guy and Nigella. Doornails. That's good. We can give the police the whole story, blame everything on her It *is* all her fault, anyway.'

'Police?' I said. 'Ravens don't go to the police . . .'

'We do if it's in our interests, Lee,' he said. 'Course we do. And if we don't they're going to be running round after you about that murder.'

At which I recalled all kinds of things. 'Billy! You nicked the book off me, you graspole. What you do that for?'

'To get the reward, dummy,' he said. 'You couldn't could you? Under the circumstances . . .'

'I didn't want the flipping reward. I wanted the book!'

'Well, I wanted the reward. And now I've got it. And have you got the book?'

'Yeah,' I said.

'So everything's OK. Let's go home.'

'Home!' I squeaked. 'I'm not going home!'

Then Janaki said, 'We should go *somewhere*. People might have noticed the crash. Might be an alarm or something.'

We stared at her. And then Billy said, 'Yeah, course.'

We splashed back to Billy's boat, past the corpse of the helicopter, past Nigella with her hair floating on the water like weed, past the first guy, who'd had the gun. Billy stared at them. I averted my gaze and told myself it wasn't my fault, it was us or them, it wasn't my fault. Janaki just stuck her nose in the air and marched by.

CHAPTER 35

Lee Again

I wasn't feeling too good to tell the truth. We reached the boat Billy had, and Janaki was on the phone to M Maggs, saying we were on our way. 'We're going to tell you everything, but we'll be tired and hungry and we have been through a lot . . . No . . . Police? Not yet, no . . . No, he' a good kid . . . He wasn't working with Nigella, not at all . . . He didn't mean to steal it! . . . Of course he didn't kil him! He had nothing to do with him . . . Listen – de Saloman didn't give the book to Nigella – Oh, you know that – Yeah but listen . . . she's dead! I know – no – no . . . Yes, we'l tell you everything . . . What? His daughter! Look – we'l come straight over as soon as we get back to London.'

There was another surprise though.

I staggered down the little steps into Billy's tiny cabin I needed to lie down.

And there was Dad.

Staring at me.

And I stared back.

'Hello there, Lee,' he said, and his face was twisted up

and for a moment I thought it was emotion at seeing me again – you know, a dad's love for his son, or something – but it wasn't. It was the same old anger.

'You little graspole,' he sneered, and his big hand came out towards me and he had me by the throat –

'LAY OFF ME!' I yelled, and I kicked and I struggled and he had thwacked me across the face and he was shouting all those things I have to block my ears against . . .

And then there was another pair of hands, and another voice, and I was lying on the floor in a heap, shuddering.

It was Billy.

He was standing above me, nose to nose with Dad. He was as tall as Dad. His muscles were as tight with fury as Dad's. He wasn't as broad as Dad, but he looked like a man.

'You,' he said, right into Dad's face. 'You stop that.'

Dad narrowed his eyes. Billy did not back down. 'You just stop it,' he said tightly. 'Now, and forever. We've had enough, Dad. All right?'

Dad blinked.

'It's time,' said Billy. 'All right? No more walloping, no more bullying, no more shouting, no more making your entire family feel like shite all the time. And if you do, *we* are going to kick *you* out of the house. All right?'

Dad blinked again.

It was a beautiful, beautiful sight. My big brother.

'I should've done this years ago,' muttered Billy.

I coughed, and struggled to my feet, and stood beside

Billy. Not to help in any fight, but to let Dad see that his sons were standing together. Together. I imagined Squidge and Ciaran with us, and even Finn. I felt great.

Actually, I felt terrible.

It was about then that everything began to go rather hazy, and my legs seemed to fall off.

It was most peculiar – I felt myself melting away from the knees. Then – BAM.

I fell over again.

I heard my dad shouting. But not in a bad way. 'Lee – Lee!' He grabbed my hand and started to swear. But not in a bad way.

He was undoing my jacket – No! But I was weak, my arms were hanging.

It was Dad on his knees beside me. Dad's hand on my hot forehead. Dad holding my wrist and counting.

'Call an ambulance,' my dad is saying. 'Now. Tell 'em suspected New Weil's disease. NOW!' Dad had me propped up against the wall, my head lolling.

I opened my eyes wide to escape the darkness which was creeping round the edges of my vision and looked around.

I tried to speak but my mouth was melting.

Janaki was on the phone. 'Suspected Weil's disease. Yes Cut on the hand – Yes, been in the sewers. Yes, he is looking a bit yellow . . .

*

I don't remember getting ashore. I don't remember the ambulance, or the hospital at Norwich, or the journey to London, or the hospital in London.

I remember waking up in a sunlit room high over a square, with Janaki sitting at the end of the bed, and Mr Maggs standing over me with a tray, and a fabulous smell of roast chicken. Janaki's eye was the one I caught, and before I could even say a word she said, 'He's under your pillow.'

I sat up and reached round. There was the touch of vellum under my fingers. Carefully, I pulled it out.

Mr Maggs was smiling at me. He put down the tray and pulled up a stool.

I looked at him and said, 'Sorry . . .'

'All's well that ends well,' he said. 'Don't worry.'

So I opened the book, and I smelt honey and oranges. I touched the page, and then I gave it to Janaki. 'Would you read to us?' I asked her.

Mr Maggs passed me the tray. 'Eat,' he said, 'before it gets cold.'

Janaki turned the page. This is what she read:

'The Book of Nebo, by the Book of Nebo, Lee the Thief, Janaki, Mr Maggs, Nigella Lurch and others.'

She looked up. Mr Maggs was staring. I was smiling.

'Chapter 1,' she continued. 'The Story According to Lee Raven, the Boy Thief. Earlier this year I got myself embroiled in an adventure so extremely peculiar and weird that if any other bloke had come up and told me it had happened to him I would've not believed him, in fact probably would've decked him for his cheek. However here I am sitting in the place to which this adventure brought me, with the purpose, prize and hero of the adventure in the hands of my friend beside me, so it must be true, and if you don't believe it I don't care because it don't matter, but don't try and deck me because if you do you'll be sorry.'

She looked up again, an expression of wonder on her face.

'Oh, don't stop,' said Mr Maggs, with a laugh. 'Please don't stop.'

So she didn't.

'I'll start at the beginning because I know that's where you ought to start a story,' she read. 'The beginning was really, all that palaver in Greek Street, Soho, London, Great Britain, the UK, 20 April 2046 . . .'

The end. Or the beginning, depending on how you look at it.